THI

Fargo's vision ... see Dandy going through the doorway and Sully holding a Smith & Wesson on her. The other one, Chester, a thin rail with a rat's face, was watching them.

Fargo whipped into motion. He swooped his right hand to his Colt and pivoted on his boot heels, thumbing back the hammer as he drew. Chester heard him and started to swing around and Fargo fanned a slug into his gut. The impact jolted Chester back a step. Gamely, Chester sought to point his revolver, and Fargo shot him again, square in the center of the sternum.

Over at the door, Sully had spun and snapped off a shot but missed.

Fargo fired as Sully went to take aim, fired as Sully stumbled, fired as Sully pitched forward and the Smith & Wesson clattered to the porch. . . .

THE TRAILSMAN

#381

BOWIE'S KNIFE

by

Jon Sharpe

A SIGNET BOOK

SIGNET
Published by the Penguin Group
Penguin Group (USA) Inc., 375 Hudson Street,
New York, New York 10014, USA

USA / Canada / UK / Ireland / Australia / New Zealand / India / South Africa / China

Penguin Books Ltd., Registered Offices: 80 Strand, London WC2R 0RL, England
For more information about the Penguin Group visit penguin.com.

First published by Signet, an imprint of New American Library,
a division of Penguin Group (USA) Inc.

First Printing, July 2013

The first chapter of this book previously appeared in *Texas Tornado*, the three
hundred seventy-seventh volume in this series.

 REGISTERED TRADEMARK—MARCA REGISTRADA

ISBN 978-0-451-41758-9

Printed in the United States of America
10 9 8 7 6 5 4 3 2 1

PUBLISHER'S NOTE
This is a work of fiction. Names, characters, places, and incidents either are the
product of the author's imagination or are used fictitiously, and any resemblance
to actual persons, living or dead, business establishments, events, or locales is
entirely coincidental.
    The publisher does not have any control over and does not assume any responsi-
bility for author or third-party Web sites or their content.

The Trailsman

Beginnings . . . they bend the tree and they mark the man. Skye Fargo was born when he was eighteen. Terror was his midwife, vengeance his first cry. Killing spawned Skye Fargo, ruthless, cold-blooded murder. Out of the acrid smoke of gunpowder still hanging in the air, he rose, cried out a promise never forgotten.

The Trailsman they began to call him all across the West: searcher, scout, hunter, the man who could see where others only looked, his skills for hire but not his soul, the man who lived each day to the fullest, yet trailed each tomorrow. Skye Fargo, the Trailsman, the seeker who could take the wildness of a land and the wanting of a woman and make them his own.

1861, the Texas border country—to get there is hard enough, to make it out alive even harder.

1

They were one day out of San Gabriel when the *bandidos* struck.

Skye Fargo had called a halt on a low rocky rise. They were in desert country, and were grateful when the heat of the day gave way to the cool of night.

Fargo wasn't expecting trouble. As their guide, it was his job to keep an eye out for hostiles and outlaws, and he'd seen nothing to suggest they were in danger.

A big man, broad at the shoulders and narrow at the hips, Fargo wore garb typical of his profession: buckskins. He was a scout by trade, although that wasn't all he did. He also wore a dusty white hat, a red bandanna, and scuffed boots. Strapped around his waist was a Colt that had seen a lot of use, and propped against the saddle next to him was a Henry rifle.

A coffee cup in his left hand, Fargo was admiring one of the members of their party over the rim.

Lustrous chestnut hair framed a pear-shaped face. She had full, luscious lips, an aquiline nose, and eyes as vivid blue as Fargo's own. Her riding outfit, which included a pleated skirt, complemented her hourglass figure and full bosom. Dandelion Caventry was her name, and just looking at her was enough to set Fargo to twitching below his belt.

"How did you get a handle like Dandelion, anyhow?" he wondered.

"I much prefer Dandy," she said in her Texas twang.

"My mother is to blame. Dandelions were her favorite flower as a little girl, so when she had one of her own . . ." Dandy grinned and shrugged.

"Thank God she wasn't fond of horseshit."

Dandy laughed heartily but the man sitting next to her didn't. He was enough like her that it was obvious they were related. He wore a tailored suit and a derby and a perpetual scowl. "You shouldn't use that kind of language in the presence of a lady."

"Horses do, you know," Fargo said.

Dandy tittered.

"That's not the point," the man said angrily. "You're much too crude for my tastes, Mr. Fargo. Much too crude by half."

"Enough, Lester," Dandy said. "I wasn't offended. And I don't need my brother to defend me."

"You shouldn't have to hear that word," Lester insisted.

Fargo shook his head in amusement. "Boy, you have a lot to learn."

"Don't call me that," Lester said. "You're not much older than I am."

"I'm old enough to say shit."

Dandy cackled but her brother became only madder. Balling his fists, Lester Caventry glanced at the two men who sat across the fire from them.

"Are you just going to sit there and let him abuse us? Am I the only one with a shred of decency?"

One of the men had a pale moon of a face and was heavyset. The other was taller with a walrus mustache. Their clothes were store-bought and far less expensive than Lester's. Each wore a bowler and each wore a revolver that his hand was always near.

"What would you have us do, Mr. Caventry?" asked the one with the moon face. Bushy brows poked from under his bowler like twin hairy caterpillars trying to crawl up his face.

"You can insist that our guide show proper manners to

my sister," Lester said. "What does my father pay you for, anyhow, Mr. Bronack? You, too, Mr. Waxler?"

"Your father," Bronack said, "is paying us to protect the two of you from any and all threats, and see to it that the knife, if it's genuine, reaches him safely."

"He never said we were to protect you from dirty words," Waxler said.

Fargo snorted.

"You don't amuse me, Mr. Waxler," Lester said. "And what could happen to the knife, anyhow?"

"Honestly, brother," Dandy said. "If it is, in fact, *the* knife, it's worth a small fortune."

"Which is what Father is willing to pay for the stupid thing," Lester said bitterly.

"Don't start with that again," Dandy said.

Fargo sighed. Ever since leaving Austin he'd had to put up with their spats. Some brothers and sisters didn't get along, and these two were always carping. To be fair, Lester did a lot more of it than Dandy. So much, in fact, several times along the way he'd been tempted to bean the sourpuss with a rock.

"I still think you should stand up for my sister's virtue," Lester directed his spite at Bronack and Waxler. "Is it too much to ask that those in our company act like gentlemen?" He gave Fargo a pointed glare.

"Honestly, brother," Dandy said.

Fargo was about to tell Lester that he could take his holier-than-thou attitude and shove it up his ass when the Ovaro raised its head and nickered.

Fargo was instantly alert. His stallion wasn't prone to skittishness. Something—or someone—was out there. Something—or someone—had agitated it. He probed the desert below the rise but saw only the ink of night.

Without being obvious about it, Fargo shifted his right arm so his hand brushed his Colt. "Bronack, Waxler," he said quietly.

The pair caught on right away. They didn't jump up in alarm. They were professionals. Each eased his hand to his six-shooter and slowly gazed about.

"What is it?" Lester asked much too loudly.

"Shut the hell up," Fargo said. "Don't move unless I say to. You and your sister, both."

"Now see here—" Lester began.

"Do as he says," Dandy intervened. "Father hired him because he's the best there is at what he does."

Fargo caught movement to the west and then to the east. Whoever was out there had the rise hemmed and was closing in. "When I tell you," he said to the Caventrys, "drop on your bellies and stay down until the shooting stops."

"What shooting?" Lester asked in confusion.

A shape rushed out of the night, the glint of a rifle in its hands. A muzzle was thrust toward them and the man shouted in Spanish, *"Nadie se mueva! Les hemos rodeado!"*

Like hell, Fargo thought. He drew as he dived and thumbed off a shot. The slug caught the man high in the chest and sent him crashing to the hard earth.

Half a dozen other shapes materialized. Rifles and pistols cracked and boomed.

Bronack and Waxler sprang to Dandy and Lester to protect them while blasting away.

Fargo saw a figure charge up and fanned two swift shots. He went for the head. Hair and brains spewed out the crown of a sombrero and the figure tumbled.

As quickly as the attack commenced, it fizzled. The rest whirled and bolted, firing a few wild shots. Their footsteps rapidly faded.

Fargo rose into a crouch. "Anyone hit?"

"I'm fine," Dandy said.

"I'm not," Lester said. "I heard one of the bullets go right past my ear."

"Did it crease you?" Dandy asked.

"No, but it scared the daylights out of me."

It was a shame, Fargo reflected, that some people gave birth to jackasses.

Bronack and Waxler straightened. Bronack was unhurt but Waxler had been nicked in the left arm. "It's nothing," he said. "I'll bandage it and be good as new."

Fargo went to the man he'd shot in the head. The grubby clothes, the stubble, the bandoleer with half the loops empty, marked him as surely as if he wore a sign. *"Bandidos."*

"Here and now?" Lester said. "Wouldn't they have been smarter to attack us in the daytime?"

"They'd have been smart to pick us off from out in the dark," Fargo said. That they hadn't was peculiar. Or maybe the bandits wanted them alive to whittle on. Except for Dandy. They'd undoubtedly put her to a different use.

"We were lucky," Bronack said.

"I can't quite believe it happened," Dandy said. "It was over so fast."

"It happened, all right." Fargo kicked the body. "Here's your proof." He went through the man's pockets but all he found was a folding knife with two blades, one of which was broken. Moving to the other one, he did the same and wound up with a handful of pesos.

"Shouldn't we douse the fire in case they come back?" Lester anxiously asked.

"They won't," Fargo said.

"How can you be so sure?"

"Three guesses." Fargo glanced at Bronack. "Keep them here and keep them quiet."

With that, staying low, Fargo glided down the rise and crouched at the bottom. He could make out some creosote and yucca, and to his left, mesquite. The bandits had fled to the south. He crept after them, careful to stop and listen often. He'd gone maybe a hundred yards when he heard what he'd hoped to hear: the drum of hooves, dwindling. He crept on and came to a wash. An acrid scent tingled his nose. At the bottom lay the stub of a smoldering cigar.

5

Fargo descended. This was where the bandits had left their mounts. Trying to follow them would be pointless. He couldn't track at night without a torch and they'd see him coming from miles off.

"Damn," Fargo said. He would have liked to show them how he felt about folks trying to kill him.

He took his time returning to the rise. It was nice to be by himself. He was tired of listening to Lester complain about everything under the sun.

Lester was a baby in a man's body. Fargo reckoned it came from being born with a silver spoon in his mouth. Their pa, Stephen Augustus Caventry, was one of the wealthiest hombres in Texas. Hell, he was one of the richest anywhere. A shipping line, a stage line, and other interests had filled his coffers to bursting.

Lester and Dandelion never wanted for anything their whole young lives. It hadn't affected Dandy much but her brother had the mistaken notion that the whole world had been created just for him.

Fargo had seldom met anyone who had their head so far up their own backside.

Another two weeks or so and he would be shed of them. That was how long it should take to reach San Gabriel, get what they came for, and light a shuck for Austin.

It had surprised him, Lester saying they were after a knife. No one had told him. Not Stephen Caventry, who'd offered him a thousand dollars to conduct his grown daughter and son to the border country and back. Not Dandy, who was friendly enough but not as friendly as he'd like. And not Lester, who gave the impression he believed they were on a fool's errand.

Fargo was so deep in thought, he'd let down his guard. The crunch of a foot behind him almost came too late. He started to turn even as a hand fell on his shoulder.

2

Fargo had his Colt out and cocked and whirled in the blink of an eye. He jammed it against the person who had grabbed his arm and he was a whisker's-width from squeezing the trigger when he realized who it was. He barely caught himself in time. "What the hell?"

Dandelion Caventry looked at his Colt and said, "Ouch." She grinned and added, "Are you fixing to shoot me?"

Fargo angrily jerked the six-shooter away and let down the hammer. "Are you trying to get yourself killed? You were supposed to stay with the others."

"I was worried about you. I came to see if you needed help."

Fargo was rattled. It had been close. So very close. "Where are your father's hired guns? Isn't one of them supposed to be keeping an eye on you?"

"Brony and Waxy heard a noise and went to investigate," Dandy said. "And they're bodyguards, not hired guns."

"Brony and Waxy?"

"It's what I like to call them." Dandy smiled and ran a hand through her full mane of hair. "I'm sorry if I startled you."

"You didn't," Fargo lied. "But grabbing me was a damn stupid thing to do."

"I didn't know if there were any bandits about or I'd have just said something."

Fargo could see there was no convincing her she'd made

a mistake that might have cost her life. She had an excuse for everything.

"Are they gone?" she asked.

"They appear to be."

Dandy grinned. "That's the most exciting thing that's happened this whole trip."

"Some kinds of excitement I can do without," Fargo said.

"I liked it," Dandy said. "It set my blood to flowing."

"Your body sets mine to flowing."

"Excuse me?" Dandy said.

"You heard me."

Dandy coughed and lost her grin. "I must say, you're forthright about it. As forthright as you are about the language you use."

"I don't beat around the bush, if that's what you mean," Fargo said. Reaching up, he touched a finger to her cheek. "This is the first chance we've had to be alone. We could go off a ways."

"Are you serious?"

"I never joke about tweaking tits," Fargo joked.

"The answer is no."

"Give it some thought. You might want to, later."

"I doubt that very much," Dandy said. "I'm not that sort of girl."

"The sort who says horseshit?"

Dandy laughed. "Don't let my brother hear you say that. He'll have a conniption."

As if that were his cue, a voice said out of the murk, "Is that you, sis?"

Lester appeared, trailed by Bronack and Waxler.

"Who else would it be, brother-mine," Dandy teased him. "Unless one of the bandits was female."

"You shouldn't have snuck off like you did, ma'am," Bronack said. "Anything happens to you, your father will blame us."

"We're paid to do a job and we wish you'd let us do it," Waxler said.

Stephen Caventry, as Fargo recollected, was in his sixties and chair-ridden thanks to an accident that cost the use of his legs. Apparently a horse he'd been riding was spooked by a rattlesnake and Caventry had taken a bad fall.

"Oh, posh," Dandy was saying. "The only danger I was in was from Mr. Fargo, here." She laughed merrily.

Fargo didn't find it nearly as humorous. Neither did her bodyguards.

"How's that again, Miss Caventry?" Bronack said.

"Did he do something he shouldn't have?" Waxler asked.

"I was joshing." Dandy poked her brother with an elbow and said, "Come on, Les. I'd like some more of those crackers before we turn in."

"I just want this whole nonsense to be over," Lester complained, trailing after her.

Fargo took a step but Bronack and Waxler moved to block his path.

"What was that about you and her?" Bronack said.

"We wouldn't want you to overstep yourself," Waxler mentioned.

"Is that a fact?" It riled Fargo that the pair were butting in where they had no business butting.

"Mr. Caventry made it quite plain about you," Bronack said. "We were hired not just to protect his son and daughter from bandits and the like. He also instructed us to protect *her* from *you*."

"That's right," Waxler said. "Mr. Caventry told us you have a reputation where the ladies are concerned."

"His exact words," Bronack said, "were that you 'like to fuck anything in skirts.'"

"Hell," Fargo said.

"Consider this a friendly warning," Waxler said.

"If that's how Caventry thinks," Fargo said, "why did he hire me?"

9

Bronack said, "The army considers you the finest scout on the frontier."

"And you have more bark on you than a redwood, as Mr. Caventry put it," Waxler said.

Fargo didn't know whether to be insulted or flattered. He decided to drop it for the time being. "Out of my way. I have coffee to finish."

The pair parted. They weren't mad at him; they were simply men doing the job they'd been hired to do.

Fargo didn't object when they fell in on either side of him.

"I have a question," Bronack said.

"So long as it's not about Dandy."

"It's about the bandits," Bronack said.

"They were stupid as stumps," Fargo said. "But most bandits are."

"You mentioned them not picking us off," Waxler brought up. "Were you suggesting they might want to get their hands on Miss Caventry?"

"Makes sense," Fargo said.

"We were wondering," Bronack said.

"Perhaps they had another reason," his partner chimed in.

"Like what?"

"Who's to say?" Bronack said.

Fargo was puzzled. What in hell could the pair be getting at? Since they were being so talkative, he asked, "What can you tell me about this knife the Caventrys are after?"

"Nothing," Bronack said.

"You don't know a thing about it?"

"We know a lot," Waxler said. "We're just not supposed to tell you."

"Mr. Caventry's orders," Bronack said.

"Wonderful," Fargo said. The more he learned, the less he realized Caventry trusted him.

"It's nothing personal," Bronack said.

"For me it is."

Waxler said, "Mr. Caventry told us because we needed to know how valuable it is."

"Or might be," Bronack added.

"A knife?" Fargo said.

"There are knives and then there are knives," Bronack said.

Dandelion and her brother were at the fire, Dandy sipping tea and eating a cracker and beaming in contentment, Lester frowning at the world and everyone in it.

Bronack made Fargo grin by saying under his breath, "Makes you wonder if they have the same father."

Fargo refilled his battered tin cup with hot coffee and sat across from Dandy so he could take up where he'd left off and admire her body. This time when he peered over the rim, her eyes met his and her cheeks became pink. But she smiled.

Lester cleared his throat. "So you say we'll reach the town of San Gabriel sometime tomorrow?"

"By noon," Fargo confirmed. "Although it's not really a town."

"Then what is it?"

"A gob of spit on the Texas side of the Rio Grande." Fargo had ridden through it once.

"I don't care how big it is," Lester said. "All I want is to inspect the damn knife and get this over with."

"Les," Dandy said, as if scolding him.

"What? I called it a knife, nothing more. And if you ask me, it will be as ordinary as wax. This is a waste of our time."

"You don't know that."

"I know Father didn't need to send me along," Lester griped. "You're the expert, not me."

"Expert?" Fargo prompted, thinking he might learn a little more.

"On antiquities," Dandy said. "I've loved old things since I was little. My grandfather's watch, my grandmother's silverware and the like fascinated me. They inspired me to collect other old things, and later to become one of the foremost antiquities dealers in Texas."

"What we're after isn't all that old," Lester said as spitefully as he said most everything else. "And what do you know about knives, anyhow?"

"I know enough to be able to determine if it's from the right time period," Dandy said. "Beyond that—" She shrugged.

"Marvelous," Lester grumped. "We might end up paying for a fake."

"It's Father's money to spend as he wants," Dandy told him.

"No," Lester said heatedly. "It's *our* money. Money he'd leave us in his will if he doesn't spend it on his pet obsession."

"I wouldn't call it that," Dandy said defensively.

"Oh, really?" Lester turned to Fargo. "I leave it to you, sir. What do you call it when someone spends every waking moment thinking and reading and talking about one thing only? What do you call it when that person is willing to spend every dollar they have on it?"

"A lot of people have hobbies," Dandy said.

"Hobbies?" Lester spat. "The Alamo isn't a hobby to him, it's—" He caught himself, and stopped.

"Consarn you," Dandy said.

"The Alamo?" Fargo said. They'd passed through San Antonio along the way, and Dandy had insisted they stop for the night and then spent hours strolling about the famous site, which the army was using as a quartermaster's depot, of all things.

Dandy glared at her brother. "Thank you for letting the cat out of the bag."

Lester didn't respond.

"My father," Dandy turned to Fargo, "is a Texan through and through. He loves this state more than anything—"

"Sometimes I suspect he loves it more than us," Lester interrupted.

"—and he's a great admirer of those who fought for Texas independence. In particular, at the Alamo. He has a whole room devoted to items of historical importance. For instance, he has a shaving kit that belonged to Travis and a powder horn that might have belonged to Davy Crockett." She paused. "Now word has reached him that someone has something that would be far and away the most important find ever, short of Crockett's rifle, Betsy."

"A knife?" Fargo said, and then it hit him. His amazement must have shown.

"Yes, *that* knife," Dandy said. "The knife that belonged to Jim Bowie."

3

Jim Bowie. The man was a legend. "Big Jim Bowie" they'd called him. He'd wielded a knife like few others, a big knife to fit the hand of a big man. A knife some say he invented, or his brother did, or a blacksmith. Whichever the case, legend had it that he had it with him at the Alamo, and when the makeshift fortress fell, the famous knife disappeared.

"You're serious?" Fargo said.

"Never more so," Dandelion replied. "Now you can see why we've kept it a secret."

No, Fargo couldn't. Sure, it was a famous knife. But he couldn't see why they were being so tight-lipped about it. "Maybe you better explain it to me."

"Don't you see? If it's genuine the knife is priceless. My father isn't the only one who would like to get his hands on it. To say nothing of the Texas government." Dandy paused and a worried look came over her. "Certain unscrupulous individuals, if they got wind that it exists, wouldn't be above trying to steal it out from under us."

"How much can it be worth?" Fargo asked skeptically.

"Again, if it's truly Bowie's, I daresay it would be appraised at half a million dollars or more."

Fargo was genuinely startled. "You have to be joshing me."

"It's Jim Bowie's *knife*," Dandy stressed.

"I say let someone else have it," Lester said.

"Ignore him," Dandy told Fargo. "As you've no doubt

noticed, he resents our father spending large sums of money. Money that could one day be ours."

"It's not right," Lester said.

"Who has this knife?" Fargo asked.

"That must remain our secret a while yet," Dandy said. "We'll reveal who it is when we get there and not before."

"Afraid I'll tell my horse?"

Dandy grinned. "I'm sorry. This is how it must be. It's not just the money involved. For a true son or daughter of Texas, the knife holds a historical value beyond measure."

Fargo supposed so. Brave men had died for the cause of Texas liberty, and the Alamo was enshrined in Texas hearts. "Remember the Alamo" had been the battle cry that brought about the defeat of Santa Anna and put Texas on the road to where it was today.

"I don't expect you to fully understand," Dandy said. "You're not a Texan, after all."

Lester fidgeted in anger. "*I'm* a Texan. But no one asks my opinion."

"You'll never let it drop, will you?" Dandy said.

"Do you want to hear my side of our argument?" Lester asked Fargo.

"No."

"Why not?"

"I don't give a damn."

Lester imitated a beet fresh out of the ground. "I resent that."

"I don't give a good damn what you resent, either."

"You can't talk to me like that," Lester said indignantly. "My father hired you, I can fire you."

"No, Les, you can't," Dandy said. "Father wouldn't want you to. And besides, what good would firing him do? Father paid him in advance. Or have you forgotten?"

"I don't like being treated as if I'm a no-account," Lester snapped.

"Then be a man and grow a pair," Fargo said.

Lester turned to their bodyguards. "Once again you two sit there and do nothing. You're next to worthless, the pair of you."

"If he tries to shoot you, we'll protect you," Bronack said.

"We can't protect you from words," Waxler said.

"He's *insulting* me," Lester almost screamed. "At the very least you should make him shut up."

"I'm sorry, Mr. Caventry," Bronack said. "Last I heard this was a free country."

"A man can speak his piece however he wants," Waxler said.

Lester pushed to his feet. "To hell with all of you." Wheeling, he scooped up his bedroll and went a dozen feet from the fire and knelt to spread it out.

"You must excuse him," Dandy said.

"Like hell," Fargo said. He didn't care for adults who never shed their diapers, and her brother was a ten-year-old in a man's body.

"Please don't hold it against him. For my sake, if for no other reason. I'd be grateful."

Fargo grinned. "*How* grateful?"

"You, sir, sink your teeth into a bone and never let go."

"I'd like to sink my teeth into something," Fargo said.

Dandy chuckled, then rose. "I suppose I better turn in too. We have a busy day ahead of us tomorrow."

"I'll take first watch," Fargo offered.

"No need," Bronack said, and motioned at Waxler. "We'll divide it up and wake you if there's cause."

Fargo let them. He'd offered before to help stand guard and they always said it wasn't necessary. It was what they were being paid for.

Rising, Fargo walked over to the Ovaro. He spread out his own blankets, and with his saddle for a pillow, lay on his back and gazed at the stars.

The night was warm and uncommonly quiet. The coyotes weren't yipping, for once.

Fargo wasn't fooled, though. Comanches could be out there. Apaches, too. Then there were the bandits, who might take it into their heads to return.

Presently, he dozed off. He slept lightly. When a fox barked, he stirred. When the throaty cough of a large cat broke the stillness, he sat up.

Waxler was at the fire. "A cougar, you reckon?"

"Jaguar," Fargo said. There was no mistaking the sound, which was more like a roar. They were rare this far north but they did stray up time to time. He stayed awake long enough to be sure it wasn't stalking their horses.

Dawn broke cool and humid.

Fargo was up before the Caventrys and put coffee on. He needed two or three cups to start his day. He also liked to end his days with two or three glasses of whiskey but he'd been bone-dry in that regard since Austin and sorely wanted to wet his throat with red-eye. He recollected San Gabriel had a cantina, thank God.

Waxler stretched and yawned. "I'll be glad to get this over with. I'm a city man at heart."

Not Fargo. Give him the wide-open spaces. The mountains, the plains, the wild places, they were his home. He could take only so much city life. A week or two at the most, and he became so restless he was fit to burst.

Waxler glanced at the sleeping forms of Dandy and Lester, and leaned toward him. "Just so you know. Their father thinks others might have heard about the knife and try to stop us from getting it or try to take it from us if we do."

Fargo appreciated the warning. "How far will these others go to get their hands on it?"

"Mr. Caventry thinks they'd kill. Which is another reason he sent Bronack and me. He'd come himself if not for his legs."

"He should have warned me," Fargo said.

"I wanted to but he said it was best to keep you in the dark. I don't know why, unless he was worried you'd want the knife for yourself."

"I have one," Fargo said. He didn't mention that it was an Arkansas toothpick in an ankle sheath in his boot.

"It's why Bronack and me wondered about those bandits," Waxler went on. "It could be they weren't bandits at all."

Fargo mulled that as he poured his first cup of coffee.

A golden arch blazed the eastern rim of the world. Soon the sun would be up and they could get under way.

Standing, Fargo stepped around to Dandy and nudged her with his boot. "Rise and shine, beautiful."

Dandy slowly raised her head and cracked those lovely eyes of hers. "Morning already?"

"Afraid so." Fargo moved to Lester and did the same, only this time he said, "Rise and shine, Nancy boy."

Lester poked his head out, his hair disheveled. "What did you call me?"

Instead of answering, Fargo reclaimed his seat.

"I thought I asked you to leave him be," Dandy said. "He can't help being how he is."

"Sure he can," Fargo said. "But he doesn't want to."

"I'm right here listening," Lester declared.

"One of us doesn't care," Fargo said.

Dandy let out a sigh. "This is no way to start the day."

"Tell me about it," Lester said. "God, I hate being here."

On that cheerful note they ate breakfast, eggs and bacon courtesy of Dandy. Their packhorse carried enough grub to last them a month.

Fargo was eager to be under way. After what Waxler had confided, he was more concerned than ever that the bandits or whoever the hell they were might come back.

As usual, Dandy and her brother took their sweet time eating. Breakfast was a ritual with them. They ate and talked. It was one of the few times during the day—any day—that Lester was halfway nice. Probably because he wasn't fully awake yet.

Fargo rarely ate breakfast, himself, when he was on the trail. Too much food made him sluggish, and in the wilds the last thing a man wanted was to be a shade slow on the draw or to not be alert in hostile country.

When Dandy offered him some eggs, though, he accepted. She had a way with a frying pan. She also rode well and never once complained, unlike her brother. For a rich gal, she was a bundle of self-reliance.

Fargo liked that in a woman. He liked how she filled out her riding outfit even more. It had been a couple of weeks since he'd been with a female, and a familiar urge was growing. Maybe that cantina would have a dove or two willing to give him a tumble.

Dandy offered eggs to the bodyguards, as well. Bronack accepted a plate and sat back down.

Waxler came over and held out his hand. "We're obliged, Miss Caventry," he said as she spooned a heaping portion out of the pan.

"How many times have I asked you to call me by my first name?" Dandy said good-naturedly. She picked up a fork. "Would you care for some bacon, too? There's plenty to go around."

Before Waxler could answer her, his face exploded.

4

The boom of the shot was nearly simultaneous with the burst of blood and brains from Waxler's head. Dead instantly, he pitched forward.

Fargo threw himself at Dandy and shoved her to the ground, covering her with his own body. Twisting, he drew his Colt and blasted a shot at the sombrero-topped man who had shot Waxler. He didn't miss.

Three other bandits materialized and more shots thundered.

Bronack unlimbered his six-gun and returned fire.

As for Lester, he squealed and flung himself flat, covering his head with his hands.

"Let me up!" Dandy protested, bucking against Fargo. "I can help."

"Stay down," he growled, and rolled off her to have a better shot at an attacker taking aim at Bronack's back. He fired first, into the bandit's chest.

Bronack shot another and the man went down.

That left a single *bandido*. He had a pistol but he wasn't much good with it. He snapped two shots at Fargo, and missed.

Fargo clipped the bandit's shoulder and was about to finish him off when a revolver cracked close to him and the top of the bandit's head imitated a geyser.

Silence fell save for the gasps of a bandit who was convulsing.

Bronack went to his partner, rolled Waxler over, and bowed his head. "Damn. He was as good a pard as I've ever had."

Fargo glanced at Dandy.

She had taken a nickel-plated, short-barreled Colt from a handbag she carried and was holding it two-handed, pointed at the bandit whose brains she had blown out.

"Nice shot."

"I've been shooting since I was ten," she replied. "I'm a Texas girl, remember?"

Fargo looked at Lester and didn't hide his disgust. "You can get up now."

"Are you sure they're dead?"

Fargo stepped to the bandit who had been convulsing but was now only twitching. Standing over him, Fargo trained the Colt. "Who hired you?"

The bandit glared.

"Quien le pago para mater?" Fargo asked.

"Bastardo," the man gasped.

"You tried to kill us, jackass. What did you expect?"

The man did more glaring.

"Por que?" Fargo said. "What were you after?"

The man sucked in a deep breath and said in English, "We were told you carry much money."

"Who told you that?"

"You will never know, gringo." The bandit grinned a bloody grin, and died.

"Damn," Fargo said.

Bronack came over, reloading his Remington. "They knew that Miss Caventry is here to buy the bowie?"

"You heard him," Fargo said. "Sounded like they did to me. Who else knew we were coming?"

"The person who has the knife," Bronack said, "and whoever they've told."

"Just what we needed."

21

"I'll bury my partner," Bronack said, "and then we can bury these others."

"Likc hell," Fargo said. "They can lie there and rot. Buzzards have to eat, too."

"That's harsh."

"The sons of bitches tried to slaughter us. They got what they deserve."

"You *do* have a lot of bark on you," Bronack said.

Fargo grunted and turned to Dandy, who was regarding her brother with contempt.

"You could have helped, Les."

"It happened so fast," Lester responded. He was still on the ground. Suddenly conscious of the fact, he quickly stood and brushed himself off. "There wasn't much I could do."

"You're a good shot," Dandy said. "We could have used your gun."

"You did well enough without me," Lester said. "Quit your carping."

"Hell, boy," Fargo said. "My piss has more backbone than you do."

Lester stopped brushing and balled his fists. "I won't be talked to like that."

"Sure you will," Fargo said, "or you'll eat your teeth."

"Skye, please," Dandy said.

"From here on out I don't give a damn what happens to your brother," Fargo informed her. "I'll look after you and only you."

"That's fine by me," Lester said. "I'm a grown man, not an infant."

"You sure?"

"And as it was my father who hired you," Lester said. "You should show me the respect I deserve."

"Good idea." Fargo was about to slug him in the gut when Dandy stepped between them.

"Please," she said.

"Out of the way."

"Must I beg?" Dandy said. "He's my brother, after all."

Fuming, Fargo wheeled and strode to the first bandit to go down. He patted each pocket and came up with a handful of pesos. The next body yielded more, and a few lucifers. The third had a folded snip of paper. On it, written in a scrawl in pencil, was *"quedarse con el dinero por si mismos."* He shoved it into one of his own pockets.

Bronack was gouging at the earth with a large rock. "This is going to take a while," he said. "Wish we had a shovel and a pick."

"We could take him with us," Fargo suggested. "Bury him in the town. It's not that far."

Bronack looked at the rock in his hand and at the hard ground, and tossed it aside. "Good idea."

Fifteen minutes more and and they had doused the fire, thrown their saddle blankets and saddles on, and were under way.

Bronack led Waxler's sorrel with Waxler's body draped over it.

Usually one or the other saw to their pack animal; Fargo thrust the lead rope at Lester Caventry.

"I don't see why I have to," he griped. "I'm not the hired help."

"Prove you're not completely worthless," Fargo said.

Taking the rope, Lester said, "I'm beginning to hate you."

They hadn't gone a quarter of a mile when the Ovaro acquired a shadow.

"You're being terribly mean to my brother," Dandy remarked. The bright sunlight seemed to lend a radiance to her face.

Fargo liked how her thighs were molded to her saddle and imagined them molded to him.

"Cat got your tongue? I said you're being mean to my brother."

"In case you haven't noticed"—Fargo was patient with

her—"your peckerwood of a brother is mean to everybody."

"I admit he can be a pain at times. But deep down he means well."

"You should lend your blinders to your horse," Fargo said.

"I've known him a lot longer than you. In a pinch he's always been there when I needed him. So I'll thank you to leave him be."

"So long as he stays out of my way."

Dandy changed the subject. "Were you surprised that the bandits came back?"

"So soon, yes," Fargo admitted. He thought of the scrap of paper in his pocket. "I've got a question for you. Do you think whoever has the knife would want to keep it as much a secret as you do?"

"I should think so, yes. It's in their best interest. Why?"

Fargo told her about the note.

"That means they knew," Dandy stated the obvious. "But I'm sure the leak wasn't at our end."

Fargo thought of Lester but said nothing. "Have you already agreed on a price?"

"Of course not. I have to examine the knife first. If it proves genuine, then, and only then, I'll make an offer."

"How high are you willing to go?"

"I'll keep that information to myself, thank you. Suffice it to say that I'll offer less than we're willing to pay and hope the seller agrees. If they don't, if they dicker, I have permission to go as high as fifty thousand dollars."

Fargo whistled.

"That's a lot of money," Dandy agreed. "But it's Jim Bowie's very own knife we're talking about."

"Wish to hell I was the seller," Fargo said, thinking of the whiskey he could drink and the doves he could bed.

"It's more than most people earn in a lifetime."

"Ten lifetimes for most," Fargo said.

"It's worth every penny to my father. He paid twelve thousand for Davy Crockett's powder horn."

Fargo whistled again. "You're sure it's Crockett's?"

"It has his initials carved into it," Dandy said. "Which I grant you isn't really proof. But Father believes it's the real article and that's what counts."

"You say he's been collecting this stuff for a while now?"

"Years. Why do you ask?"

"A lot of people must know he does."

"I see what you're implying. That if it's so well known, unscrupulous individuals might try to take advantage of him."

"When it comes to greed, people will do all sorts of things."

"True. One man claimed to have a coat that belonged to Travis, complete with his initials on the collar. But the ink wasn't in use back in 1836. I easily exposed him as a fraud."

"Who's to say the knife isn't, too?"

"That's what Father is relying on me to determine," Dandy said with noticeable pride.

"What's your brother's part in this? Besides bitching?"

"Believe it or not, he came along to keep me company."

"And cows fly," Fargo said.

"Be nice. Les and I spat a lot but deep down he cares for me and I care for him."

"If you say so."

"I do. And as a favor to me, be more civil to him."

"Civil, hell," Fargo said. "But for you I'll try." Especially if it helped persuade her to shed her clothes some day or night soon.

"You're a dear," Dandy said sweetly.

"That's me," Fargo said. "Dear as can be."

5

San Gabriel was as lively as a turtle. The lone dusty street was empty of life save for a rooster and several hens. A dog lay in the shade of an overhang, dozing.

There was the *cantina* Fargo remembered, along with a small general store, a livery, and a dozen or so dwellings. Most of the buildings were adobe.

The hitch rail in front of the *cantina* was empty. Fargo drew rein, alighted, and wrapped the reins.

"What are you doing?" Dandy asked. "The person we need to see has a ranch outside of town."

"You never told me," Fargo said.

"Climb back on and we'll be on our way."

"I aim to wet my throat first," Fargo said. And with a little luck, maybe treat himself to something more.

"I insist," Dandy insisted.

Fargo was about to reply that she could insist until she was blue in the face and he was still going to have a drink but Bronack spared him the trouble by coughing to get her attention and motioning at the sorrel and his partner's body.

"You're forgetting Waxler, ma'am. I'd like to see that he's planted proper before we go on to the ranch."

"Oh," Dandy said. "Yes, of course."

"I'll ask around about the cemetery. Then the undertaker, if they have one, will need to measure him for a coffin. It will take a while," Bronack said.

"I suppose it can't be helped."

Lester had been unusually quiet all morning. Now he stiffly dismounted and looped his reins. "Let's take a stroll around this dustbin, sis. I can stand to stretch my legs."

"All right. We'll all meet back here in an hour's time," Dandy informed them. "Don't be late."

Fargo butted the batwings with a shoulder and ambled over to the bar. The place smelled of liquor and cigar smoke.

An old man was asleep at a table, an empty bottle in front of him.

"Can I help you, *senor*?" the bartender asked. He had little hair to speak of and a huge belly. Taking a dirty towel from his shoulder, he wiped the bar. It didn't clean it so much as rearrange the grime.

"Monongahela if you have it," Fargo said, moving around a spittoon that hadn't been cleaned in a coon's age.

The bartender selected a bottle, wiped the mouth on his sleeve, and brought it over, along with a glass with smudge marks. "Here you are, *senor*."

"I don't need the glass," Fargo informed him. He wiped the bottle on his own sleeve, tilted it to his mouth, and took several gulps. A warm sensation filled his belly, and spread. "Good red-eye."

The bartender grinned in gratitude. "I think so, too. Most of my customers would rather have tequila though."

"Is there much to do around here besides watch the grass grow?" Fargo asked. Not that he'd seen much grass on his way in.

"There's Consuelo. She has a room at the back but she doesn't usually come out until sundown. Her nights are very busy." The bartender winked.

"Does she like whiskey?"

"She loves it almost as much as she loves men." The bartender gave him another wink.

With the bottle in hand, Fargo went along a musty hall until he came to a door. He knocked, and when there was no answer, he knocked louder.

"Quien es?" a female voice asked.

"A randy goat," Fargo admitted. "Open up."

"It is too early yet. Go away."

"I'll treat you to a bottle."

"Didn't you hear me, *senor*? I will be out when the sun goes down, not before."

"I'll be gone by then," Fargo said. "And here I was willing to pay you double what you usually ask—" That last came to him in a burst of inspiration.

"Espere, por favor."

Fargo waited. He heard rustlings and shuffling and the next moment he was enveloped in perfume. He didn't know what he expected but it certainly wasn't the vision the doorway framed. She wasn't much over twenty, with gorgeous black hair, watermelons above her waist and shapely thighs below. None of which was concealed by the lacy gown she had thrown on. "Consuelo, is it?"

She raked him from hat to boots and puckered her full lips. "Oh my. You said you were a goat but I think you are more like a bull." The pink tip of her tongue poked out. "I do so like bulls."

"And I like big tits so we're even." Fargo held out the bottle. *"Cuidar a un trago?"*

"Don't mind if I do. *Gracias.*" Consuelo took the bottle and swigged without batting an eyelash. Smiling, she dabbed at her mouth and handed the bottle back. "Give me a few minutes to make myself presentable, as you gringos would say."

Fargo fixed his gaze on her breasts. "You're fine as you are."

"Please, *senor.* I will touch up a little."

Fargo shrugged. Some females were fussier than others when it came to their appearance. "I'll be at the bar."

Two men were there who hadn't been before, at the far end. Both wore sombreros and had pistols high on their hips.

"She said no?" the bartender asked, sounding surprised.

"She needs to spruce up first," Fargo said.

"Spruce up?" The bartender scratched his head, then smiled. "Oh. *Si*. She will be worth the wait, I promise you." He glanced at the pair at the far end and said under his breath so that Fargo barely heard, *"Espero que no hay ningun problema."*

"You hope there is no trouble?" Fargo translated. "Why would there be?"

Before the bartender could answer, out came Consuelo. She hadn't taken nearly as long as she said she would. She wore a red dress, and from the way it clung to her body, Fargo doubted she had anything on underneath.

"That was quick," he said.

"For a handsome man like you—" Consuelo began, and stopped when she saw the two at the end of the bar. Her smile became a grimace.

"Something the matter?" Fargo asked.

"I hope not."

The pair came toward them, the large rowels on their spurs jingling with every step. Ignoring Fargo, they stopped in front of Consuelo.

"We have come for you, woman," one said in Spanish.

"Tadeo, Basilio," Consuelo said, and bobbed her chin at Fargo. "Can't you see I'm busy? Come back in an hour. Or better yet, two."

"We were told to bring you pronto," the one called Tadeo said. He had a cleft chin and a small scar on his cheek.

"You will come with us now," Basilio said, and grasped her wrist.

"Please. Let go," Consuelo said.

Fargo had noticed an empty glass on the bar near his elbow. Filling it from his bottle, he said, "You heard the lady. She's busy."

"This doesn't concern you, gringo," Basilio said in Spanish.

"If you want to stay healthy, stay out of it," Tadeo threw in.

"Por favor," Consuelo said to them. "Surely an hour won't matter?"

"Pronto means right away," Tadeo said, pulling on her arm.

"I won't go," Consuelo said.

"Quit being foolish, woman," Basilio said. "You are to come and that is all there is to it."

"I'd leave the lady be," Fargo suggested.

"Wd told you to butt out, gringo," Tadeo snapped.

"We will not tell you again," Basilio said.

"Do your *madres* know they raised jackasses?" Fargo asked. Before they could answer, he swept the glass in an arc with his left hand even as he stabbed his right hand for his Colt.

The whiskey caught both in the face. They recoiled and plunged their hands for their own hardware but neither had cleared leather when the click of the Colt's hammer turned them to stone.

"Madre de Dios," the bartender exclaimed.

Fargo took a step away from the bar so he had room to move. "You can die or you can light a shuck. Your choice."

"You are fast, gringo," Basilio said. "Very fast."

"So are we," Tadeo said, whiskey dripping from his chin. "You can't drop both of us."

"Care to bet?" Fargo said.

Tadeo tensed as if to go for his pistol but Basilio nudged him and shook his head.

"No. Ahora no."

"Se le puede ganar," Tadeo said.

"No, I say," Basilio said in English. Smiling at Fargo, he began to back away, his hands splayed out from his sides. "We are leaving, gringo."

Reluctantly, Tadeo backed off, too, but his hand was poised to draw. "This isn't over."

"If you're smart it is," Fargo said.

The batwings creaked and the jangling of their spurs faded.

"Thank God," the bartender said. "I thought for sure they would spill blood."

"Someone would," Fargo said. He twirled the Colt into his holster, picked up the bottle, and took a healthy pull. Setting it down, he turned to Consuelo and grinned. "Now where were we?"

6

Fargo liked women who liked it as much as he did.

Consuelo liked it a lot. Once they reached her room, she melted into him, kissing, groping, caressing, massaging .

The room was small but comfortable. Curtains adorned a window and a rug covered the floor. The bed was a surprise: a four-poster with a flowered quilt.

At the first touch of her hand below his belt, Fargo felt himself swell.

"Oh, my," Consuelo husked in his ear. "You are *grande*, yes?"

"Ever seen a redwood?" Fargo said.

It fired her hunger. Eagerly, she drew him to the bed and clawed at his buckskins as if fit to rip them off.

As Fargo had suspected, she didn't have anything on under her dress. Once he'd peeled it from her luscious body, she lay on her back with a leg crooked in invitation. She was exquisite to behold: full, ripe breasts, their tips rigid as nails; a flat tummy and a bushy thatch; and creamy thighs that went on forever.

Fargo got a constriction in his throat just looking at her. He ran his hands everywhere and roamed his mouth over her tits and her stomach and up to her ear. Her lobe was sensitive and she arched her back when he licked and nipped it.

It wasn't long before Consuelo became an inferno of desire. She was especially fond of cupping him down low and running her hand his entire hard length. It made him shiver.

At the back of his mind Fargo didn't forget he was supposed to meet up with Dandy and the others. After about ten minutes of foreplay, he eased to his knees between Consuelo's legs, spread her wide, and went to penetrate her.

Consuelo, smiling hungrily, pushed his hand away to do it herself. Uttering tiny mews of pleasure, she fed him in inch by gradual inch, her eyes widening toward the end. "There is so much of you," she breathed. "I love it."

"Do tell," Fargo said. He stroked just once, lifting her bottom off the bed.

"Ahhh!" Consuelo moaned. Digging her fingernails into his shoulders, she bit him. "Do it, *senor*. Do it rough."

Fargo propped his hands on either side of her and became a living piston, driving up and in, up and in, each thrust inciting her more.

Consuelo cooed and kissed and gooaned and caressed and reached the summit before he did. She crested with a cry of rapture, her thighs clamping tight as her tunnel burst with moisture. She gushed and gushed, an upheaval that would do justice to an earthquake. At last she subsided and lay limp and satiated, saying, "That was magnificent."

"We're not done."

Her eyes widened anew as Fargo resumed his rhythm, rocking on his knees and his hands. Her inner sheath was a wet glove that heightened his pleasure.

He was at it a good long while. She came again and was on the verge of a third time when he felt himself about to explode.

Consuelo sensed it, too. "Make me scream," she said.

Fargo did. Afterward, they lay on their sides facing each other. He was slick with sweat and fully relaxed for the first time in days. "*Gracias*," he said.

"No, thank *you*," Consuelo said breathlessly. "You are one of the best ever."

"I bet you say that to all the bulls," Fargo joked. He closed his eyes, tempted to doze off. But no, if he did, he'd keep Dandy and the others waiting. Fighting the urge off, he slowly sat up and leaned back against the headboard.

"You are leaving already?" Consuelo asked.

"I have to," Fargo said. "Damn it."

"Come visit me again, yes? I would like that very much." Consuelo placed the tip of a finger on his gut and moved it in slow circles, lower each time.

"No, you don't," Fargo said, grinning. He slid off before she got him hard again, and put himself together. His boots were last, and as he tugged them on, she played with his hair and his ear.

"I am sorry to see you go. You are great fun."

"Tell me something," Fargo thought to ask. "How long have you been here?"

"About five years now. Why?"

"Ever hear of someone who has a knife that supposedly belonged to James Bowie?"

"Bowie? The knife-fighter from the Alamo? I have not, no," Consuelo said. "I hear a lot of gossip, thanks to my work. But I have never heard that."

"You call this work?" Fargo teased, and gave her fanny a swat.

Consuelo squealed in delight. "Men like to talk when they are through. They tell me about their wives, their families, their lives. It bores me but they pay me so I endure it."

"Speaking of pay," Fargo said, and reached for his poke.

"No, handsome one," Consuelo said, placing her hand on his. "That is not necessary."

"I don't mind," Fargo said.

"I do. This time was for me. For the fun of it, as you gringos say."

"Suit yourself." Fargo kissed her, and stood. He strolled out at peace with the world until he got to the main room.

They were back. Basilio was to the right of the batwings, Tadeo to the left, their thumbs hooked in their gun belts.

"Some folks," Fargo said, "have no brains."

"We are not here for you," Basilio said. "Only to take the woman to someone who wants her company."

"Speak for yourself," Tadeo said. "I would try this gringo if not for you."

"You are too hot-blooded," Basilio said, "and are to do as I say." He moved away from the doorway.

Swearing bitterly in Spanish, Tadeo, too, backed off.

Fargo's bottle was still on the bar. He snagged it with his left hand and walked out, careful not to turn his back to Tadeo as he shoved through the batwings.

The horses at the hitch rail had hung their heads from the heat. Down the street, Bronack emerged from a building with a small man in a dark suit, shook the man's hand, and came toward the *cantina*.

Fargo leaned against the front wall and treated himself to more whiskey. A single bottle wouldn't get him drunk, as it did most men. It took two or three.

"All taken care of," Bronack said when he was close enough. "That was the undertaker." He looked around. "Seen any sign of Miss Caventry and her brother?"

Fargo shook his head.

"I shouldn't have left them alone," Bronack said. He dug a pocket watch from his vest and flipped the cover open. "It hasn't been an hour yet so maybe that's why."

Fargo held out the bottle.

"I shouldn't." But Bronack took a light swallow and gave the bottle back.

"That's all?"

"I'll get good and drunk when I get back to Austin. Not before." Bronack glanced sharply to the north. "Here they come. It looks like they're arguing."

"When don't they?" Fargo said.

Dandelion and Lester were at it again, with Lester doing a lot of angry gesturing. His sister, unruffled, kept shaking her head.

"They remind me of my niece and nephew," Bronack said, "who are eight and ten years old."

Fargo chuckled.

The siblings neared the hitch rail. Lester was red in the face and looked ready to spit nails.

"What is it this time?" Fargo asked.

"None of your business," Lester snapped.

"He wants me to offer less for the bowie than Father told us to," Dandy said, "and keep the difference for ourselves."

"Why not?" Lester said. "As I keep having to remind you over and over, it's our inheritance he's squandering."

"I'm so tired of you going on about that," Dandy said. "It's not really ours until Father dies, and he could live a good twenty years yet. Who knows how much money he'll have to pass on by then?"

"That's exactly my point," Lester said. "I don't intend to let him deprive me of what's rightfully mine."

"God, Les."

"Don't God me, consarn you."

Maybe it was tangling with the *pistoleros* or maybe it was the heat and the whiskey, but Fargo had reached the end of his patience. Striding over to Lester, he poked him in the chest so hard, Lester almost fell. "Not another goddamn word about your goddamn inheritance."

Lester was incredulous. "You can't talk to me like that."

"I'll do a hell of a lot more than talk if you don't shut the hell up."

"Skye, no," Dandy said softly.

"You have to put up with him because he's your brother," Fargo said. "I don't. If he annoys me just one more time—"

Lester turned to Bronack. "You're standing right there. You had to hear him threaten me. Yet once again you do nothing."

"He hasn't gone for his gun," Bronack said.

"I'll remember this," Lester fumed. "I'll tell Father and have you fired. Just see if I don't."

Dandy stepped to her horse. "Enough. Let's be on our way. With a little luck we can conclude our business by nightfall and head home."

The road was an inch thick with dust and pockmarked with hoofprints. On both sides stretched grassland, the grass mostly brown from the summer heat. A lone belt of green along the Rio Grande was the exception.

Fargo was in the lead, his hand on his Colt. Whoever had sent the bandits might send others.

Dandy brought her bay up next to the Ovaro. "Did you enjoy that run-down little hole of a saloon?" she sarcastically asked.

"It was a nice hole," Fargo said.

"Now that we're almost there, it's only fair I warn you," Dandy said. "The person we're going to see, the person who claims to have the bowie, has a reputation for being vicious when their ire is aroused."

"People have ires?" Fargo said.

"Poke fun if you must. But be on your best behavior when we get there. I don't want you to ruin my father's chance to buy the knife."

"If anyone will ruin it," Fargo said, "it's your brother."

"Even he wouldn't dare make her mad."

"Her?"

Dandy frowned. "I might as well reveal the rest. Her name is Patterson. Sarah Patterson. Most in these parts know her by her nickname."

"Which is?" Fargo prompted when she didn't go on.

"The Throat Slitter."

7

As Dandy related it, Sarah Patterson had married into money. Not once or twice but three times. Her latest conquest had been rough-and-tumble Charlie Patterson, owner of the Bar P, one of the largest ranches in all of Texas.

Patterson had been pushing fifty. He was too busy in his earlier years establishing his cattle empire to give any thought to getting hitched. Then one day he went on a trip to Houston and met Sarah.

The cynical had it that she played him like a fiddle and wrapped him around her little finger. The cynical were probably right. Before Charlie left Houston, they were engaged. Before six months had gone by, they were hitched. Sarah moved in to Charlie's sprawling ranch house and immediately took over.

"All that's fine and dandy," Fargo interrupted. "But how did she get the nickname of Throat Slitter?"

"I'm coming to that," Dandy said.

Apparently Sarah had become very protective of the Bar P. Even more than Charlie. Their ranch bordered another on the Mexican side, the Alante spread, and when some *vaqueros* pushed their cattle onto the Bar P, claiming the land was Alante's, Charlie and his punchers, and Sarah, paid their camp a visit.

Fargo grunted in surprise. It was rare for a man to take his wife along on something like that. Range disputes often resulted in gunplay.

"No one ever saw those *vaqueros* again," Dandy revealed. "Alante sent word to Charlie Patterson that it was a mistake and assured Patterson nothing like that would ever happen again."

"Men can't just vanish," Fargo said.

"It's just a rumor, mind you, but my father says that Charlie explained to the *vaqueros* that they were on his land and asked them to herd their cattle back where it belonged. They refused. Charlie was still trying to reason with them when Sarah ordered the Bar P hands to jump them and hold them down. Supposedly eight *vaqueros* were taken alive." Dandy paused. "Sarah went from one to the next and slit their throats."

"Charlie Patterson did nothing?"

"The word is that Charlie was very much afraid of her. When she invited *Senor* Alante to their ranch for a parley, he went along with it. And then stood by and did nothing when she had her men hold Alante down so she could slit his throat, too."

"The hell you say."

"The Alante spread became part of the Bar P. Charlie died about three years ago and Sarah has had the ranch to herself ever since. She hasn't remarried. My father met her once. He told me she runs the Bar P like a queen, and anyone who crosses her regrets it."

"*This* is the woman who has Bowie's knife?"

"She claims she does, yes. She sent her ramrod, a gentleman called Brazos, to contact my father, and here we are."

"How did she get hold of it?"

"We don't know. The ramrod said she had heard Father was interested in Alamo artifacts and she was offering it to him first but if he wasn't interested, she'd find another buyer."

"I'd have made her bring the knife to me."

"She never leaves the Bar P these days. Or so her foreman assured us." Dandy gazed in the direction they were riding. "Father couldn't think of any reason she would try to dupe him. It's not as if she needs the money."

It was another hour and a half before the rutted road brought them to a sign made of logs and planks. BEYOND THIS POINT IS BAR P LAND, it read. NO TRESPASSING ALLOWED. RUSTLERS WILL BE HUNG. DRUMMERS WILL BE TARRED AND FEATHERED.

"Friendly place," Fargo said.

They no sooner passed the sign than two young cowboys rode up out of a dry wash to bar their way. Both wore chaps and pistols, and the taller of the two demanded, "Who are you and what's your business on the Bar P?"

"I'm Dandelion Caventry," Dandy explained. "Your mistress sent for us."

"Caventry?" the tall puncher said. "Then you'd be the knife lady?"

"I would."

"I'm to take you to the ranch house when you show up. These others have to stay here."

"Out of the question," Dandy said.

"Ma'am, those orders are straight from Mrs. Patterson herself."

"All four of us go or none of us do," Dandy said. "Send word to her and we'll wait."

"It'd be three days before I got back," the tall puncher said. "You want to wait that long?"

"You're joshing."

"Ma'am, this is the Bar P. It takes ten days to ride across it from end to end It'll take a day and a half just to to reach the ranch house and a day and half to come back."

"I had no idea." Dandy pondered and said, "I don't care. We'll make camp and wait. I'm not leaving my brother. And these other two go with us or we don't go at all."

The cowboys consulted in low tones and the tall puncher frowned and cleared his throat.

"All right, ma'am. I'll likely as not get in trouble with

the boss. But she did say I wasn't to waste time fetching you."

"I'll speak to her on your behalf," Dandy offered.

"That's kind of you, ma'am," the tall man said, "but you don't know her like I do."

They rode hard. Fargo lost count of the cattle they saw. A fortune on the hoof.

That night they camped by a spring. The punchers sat by themselves and didn't say much. Lester was in one of his sulks. Bronack hadn't gotten over Waxler and spent the evening staring into his coffee cup. Even Dandy was unusually quiet.

"Sure is a lively bunch," Fargo remarked.

"I have a lot on my mind," Dandy said. "I'm hoping everything goes well so I can justify Father's faith in me."

"You need to relax," Fargo suggested. "How about if we go for a stroll?"

"Just the two of us? Alone in the dark?" Dandy shook her head, but grinned. "You never give up, do you?"

"As easy on the eyes as you are," Fargo said, "you can't blame me."

"Flattery, sir, will get you nowhere," Dandy teased. "It's not as if men haven't tried all kinds of ways before."

"Here's one I bet you haven't heard." Fargo bent so no one else would hear. "We go for a walk, do what comes naturally, and sleep like babies the rest of the night."

Dandy had a marvelous laugh. "I would accuse you of being a cad but I know you're just being playful."

"You see right through me," Fargo said. The hell of it was, he was serious. But since he wasn't going to get up her dress, he announced that he'd keep first watch if the rest wanted to turn in.

The punchers were the first to spread their bedrolls. Bronack was next, saying he'd relieve Fargo at midnight. Lester sat in his usual perpetual sulk but finally he lay down and pulled a blanket over his head.

That left Dandy. She sat and doodled in the dirt with a stick.

"Not tired?" Fargo said.

"I'm too wrought up. If I'm wrong about the knife, I could cost my father a lot of money for nothing."

"It's not as if he can't spare it."

"That's not the point. He trusts me." She rubbed her shoulder, and winced. "My body is in knots, I'm so tense."

"I can untie them for you."

"No."

"How about I give you a backrub? That should help."

"Your hands," Dandy said, "are not touching my body. And that's final."

"I have some whiskey left."

"That's generous of you. But again, no. It would lower my inhibitions, which is exactly what you want."

"Me?" Fargo said innocently.

Dandy chortled.

"So, do we go for a walk?"

"Do you *ever* take no for an answer?"

Fargo scratched his chin as if thinking. "No."

"I think I'll turn in before you talk me out of my chemise."

"I'm obliged," Fargo said.

"For what?"

"Giving me hope."

"I did no such thing."

"You haven't slapped me."

"You, sir, are incorrigible."

"Mostly I'm horny."

Dandy started to laugh loudly but glanced at the others and covered her mouth with her hand. She went around the fire, laid out her blankets, smiled, and turned in.

"Hell," Fargo said.

The night was quiet save for the occasional lowing of cattle and the cries of coyotes.

At one point Fargo shifted and stretched and happened to spot the orange glow of another campfire. He made it to be a mile ahead, or better. Punchers, he figured. The Comanches and the Apaches wouldn't make their fire where it could be seen. And bandits weren't about to dare the wrath of a tough outfit like the Bar P.

Midnight came, and it was Bronack's turn.

Fargo slept fitfully. He tossed. He turned. He had no reason to be restless, yet he was. Daybreak couldn't come soon enough. He was the first to saddle his horse and the first in the saddle when everyone was ready to head out.

The punchers led. They drew rein when they came to the smoldering embers of the fire Fargo had noticed the night before.

"Must be the greasers," the shorter of the cowboys said. "I don't much like that she uses them and not any of us."

"I don't know why she does it, either, but they work for her the same as we do," the tall puncher said.

"Even so."

On that mysterious note they rode on.

The closer they grew to the ranch house, the more cowhands they saw. Most, Fargo noticed, were as young as their escorts. That struck him as strange. A lot of ranches preferred more seasoned hands.

They came to a low ridge that overlooked a dozen outbuildings and the house.

"Dear Lord," Dandy exclaimed. "Tell me I'm dreaming."

Fargo summed up his astonishment with, "I'll be damned."

8

The buildings, every last one, were painted pink. The ranch house, the stable, pink. The bunkhouse, the blacksmith's shop, pink. Even a chicken coop and the outhouses, pink.

"It's the boss lady's doing," the tall puncher explained. "The week after her husband passed on, she sent for the paint."

"It sort of grows on you after a while," the other cowhand said.

Fargo looked at him.

"A long while," the cowhand amended.

"Mrs. Patterson wanted to liven up the spread," the tall puncher said, his cheeks almost as pink as the buildings. "Make it more female, as she put it."

"More female?" Fargo said.

"When you meet her, you'll savvy."

"You punchers didn't mind?"

"Two or three of the older ones packed their wag bags and lit out. They said it wasn't natural, making everything pink. The rest of us stayed on. And like Shorty just told you, you get used to it."

"Not in a hundred years," Fargo said.

"Well, I think it's perfectly adorable," Dandy said. "My bonnet is off to her."

Lester roused from his sulk to say, "I see a lot of pink things when I'm drunk." He smacked his lips. "I wish I was drunk now."

So did Fargo.

"Come on," the tall cowboy said. "And I hope she doesn't skin me alive."

Cowboys were at the corral, cowboys were busy at the stable, cowboys were scattered here and there. About half wore sombreros. Most stopped what they were doing to stare.

"Do you suppose it's me?" Dandy asked.

"Probably Lester," Fargo said.

"I heard that," Lester said.

A well-watered yard shaded by oaks and rimmed by a pink picket fence fronted the house, which was three stories high and three times as long as most ranch houses Fargo had seen.

They no sooner drew rein at a hitch rail next to a gravel path than a handsome young man in a black jacket and pants came out on the broad porch.

"Miquel, we need to see the boss lady," the tall puncher said.

"I will tell her, *Senor* Clay."

Fargo was glad to climb down and stretch. They had been riding for so many days, his kinks had kinks.

Clay and Shorty ushered them along a path to the stairs. Bronack came last, his right hand hooked in his belt near his Remington.

Fargo didn't see cause for alarm. None of the hands acted unfriendly.

Then the front door opened, and Fargo almost whistled in admiration.

Sarah Patterson was thirty if she was a day. Her hair was a rich brown, her body didn't show an inch of "wide" anywhere. She had on a pink dress and pink earrings. And no doubt about it, she was an eyeful. In every respect she appeared to be the perfect lady. Until she opened her mouth. "What the hell is this, Clay? It better be goddamned important to bring me out in this heat." Her eyes, an emerald green, flashed with fire.

45

"It's the knife gal, Mrs. Patterson," Clay replied. "I brung her like you wanted."

Sarah Patterson gave Dandy a strange sort of scrutiny. "So this is her? Who are these others? I told you her and her alone."

Dandy said, "It's my doing, Mrs. Patterson. I couldn't very well leave my brother and . . ."

"I'll get to you in a minute, dearie," Sarah interrupted. She jabbed a finger at Clay. "I don't like being disobeyed. You know that. I have half a mind to fire you."

Fargo never could abide obnoxious people. "Do your ears work or are you just a bitch?"

Everyone stiffened.

Sarah Patterson slowly turned, and if her green eyes were fire before, now they were molten lava. "*What* did you just call me?"

"A bitch," Fargo said. "Miss Caventry was talking to you and you ignored her."

"Who the hell are you?"

"The gent who brought these folks here and can take them right back if this is how you're going to treat them."

"Skye, no," Dandy whispered.

Clay and Shorty were dumbfounded. Miquel appeared terrified.

Sarah Patterson took a step, and stopped. The fury on her face faded and was replaced by something else. "Well, now," she said, appraising him much as a horse-buyer might appraise a stallion. "Who do we have here?"

Fargo introduced himself. He also introduced Bronack but she didn't so much as acknowledge he existed.

"Has anyone ever told you that you're awful easy on the eyes?" Sarah asked in a throaty purr that hadn't been there a moment ago. She smiled at Dandy. "So are you, sweetie."

Dandy seemed puzzled. "I'm what now?"

"I reckon I did jump out of the gate," Sarah said to Fargo. "Thank you for bringing me to my senses."

"About the knife—" Dandy said.

"Please, you just got here," Sarah said. "Business can wait until after you're refreshed and we've had a talk." She came down the steps and hooked her arm with Fargo's. "How about if I take you to the sitting room and serve coffee or tea?"

"Tea, hell," Fargo said. "Do you have any whiskey?"

Sarah Patterson squeezed his arm. "Handsome, I have every kind of liquor, and then some. You're welcome to whatever you want." She looked down at her own body. "*Whatever* you want," she stressed.

Miquel moved aside and Sarah guided Fargo toward the house, pausing to say over her shoulder, "Clay? Shorty? Why are you two still here? You have jobs to do."

The pair looked relieved.

"Yes, ma'am," Clay said. "We'll be on our way."

Sarah ran her hand up Fargo's arm. "My, what nice muscles you have."

"Are you always so friendly?" Fargo asked.

"I like my treats. It's how I hooked Charlie and my other husbands."

"Treats?" Fargo said.

Sarah Patterson glanced at his crotch. "We're all fond of something."

Fargo liked her honesty. He liked, too, how her bodice swelled, and the suggestion of willowy legs under her dress.

Behind them Dandy said, "Mrs. Patterson, I really would like to talk about Jim Bowie's knife."

"Honestly, sweetie," Sarah said. "It can wait until supper. In the meantime we'll get better acquainted."

The interior put most ranches to shame. Extravagant, was how Fargo would describe it. Paneling and carpet and all the little luxuries, like a chandelier, of all things, in the sitting room. He roosted on a settee. Lester plopped into a chair while Bronack leaned against a wall.

"Miquel, a whiskey for this handsome gentleman," Sarah commanded. "And whatever else my guests desire." She smiled and gave a slight bow. "If you'll excuse me, I'll be right back." Out she whisked.

"Goodness," Dandy said. "She's not at all as I expected her to be."

"Are we staying the night?" Lester asked.

"Most likely. She doesn't seem in any rush and we have a lot to discuss. Why?"

"I've only just met her and I dislike her."

"You would."

Staying the night was fine by Fargo. He'd like to find out if the mistress of the house was even friendlier after the sun went down.

Lester was saying, "The woman is rude. She hasn't spoken three words to me."

"Don't jump to conclusions," Dandy said.

Just then a dress rustled and a woman entered. But it wasn't Sarah Patterson.

Fargo almost thought he was imagining things. "Consuelo?" he said, coming to his feet.

Consuelo drew up short. "Skye? What are you doing here? Did you follow me?"

"You know this woman?" Dandy asked.

"I came with these people," Fargo answered Consuelo. She was wearing an expensive sea-blue dress and her hair practically glistened. He remembered the campfire they had seen the night before, ahead of their own. "Is this where Basilio and Tadeo brought you?"

Consuelo nodded. "She sends for me from time to time. She pays very well."

"No," Fargo said.

"Yes," Consuelo said.

"I'll be damned."

"What are you two talking about?" Dandy asked. "If it's any of my business?"

"How friendly Sarah Patterson is," Fargo said.

"She is, isn't she? All those stories I heard must be exaggerated. She's a lot nicer than everyone makes her out to be."

Consuelo came over to Fargo and rose on her toes so her mouth was at his ear. "I am sorry to see you here."

"Why?" Fargo asked in surprise.

"Be on your guard. Mrs. Patterson, she is loco. You can never predict what she will do."

"You seem safe enough," Fargo said.

Consuelo gripped his hand so hard, it hurt. "Please believe me. She has no boundaries, this one. No boundaries at all."

"Boundaries?" Fargo said.

Just then Sarah returned. "Consuelo, there you are. I wanted to tell you I have company and you should stay in your room but now you might as well join us."

"I would like that," Consuelo said, stepping away from Fargo. *"Muchas gracias."*

Sarah turned toward the easy chair, and Lester. "So you're the brother? You don't say much, do you? Must come from being so scrawny."

"I'll thank you not to insult me," Lester said, sitting up.

"The truth is never an insult." Sarah smiled at Dandy. "It's plain your sister got all the looks in your family."

"Mrs. Patterson, please," Dandy said modestly.

"I don't like you much, lady," Lester said.

"I'll try not to lose sleep over it." Sarah turned back to Dandy. "Sorry to be so rude to him, my dear, but your brother is a cockroach."

Fargo laughed.

"He can be quite pleasant when he puts his mind to it," Dandy said.

"How about you, sweetie? What do you like to put your body to?"

"I beg your pardon?"

Sarah turned yet again, to Fargo. "I promised you a whiskey, didn't I? My husband, God rest him, liked the most expensive brands. I'll have the maid bring a bottle and a tray." She raised the hem of her dress, displaying shapely ankles. "I also need to give instructions to the cook." Out she whisked.

"Goodness gracious," Dandy said. "She's like a dragonfly, flitting this way and that."

"More like a wasp, *senorita*," Consuela said. "The kind that stings."

"Why do you say that? She's being as nice as she can be."

Consuelo gave a slight bow. "Believe as you will. If you will excuse me, I must freshen up before supper."

"Will I see you later?" Fargo asked.

"Not under her roof," Consuelo said. "I do not want to be stung." She smiled and departed.

"What a strange woman. I don't quite know what to make of all this," Dandy remarked. Brightening, she said, "It promises to be an interesting evening, though, don't you think?"

"In more ways than one," Fargo said.

9

Sarah Patterson lived the life of a queen. She had servants to wait on her hand and foot. She had cowhands eager to please to do the work around the part of her ranch that was north of the border and *vagueros* to do the same for the part of the Bar P that was south of the border.

Her dinner table was longer than a keelboat. Fine china glittered, silverware gleamed. In addition to Miquel, a Mexican girl in a skimpy outfit by the name of Lupe and a man of middling years in a starched uniform were at her beck and call during the meal.

Dandy and even Lester seemed to be in awe of her.

Fargo wasn't. He never did take to people who put themselves on pedestals. The way she spoke to her servants, the way she held herself, suggested she looked down her nose at most everyone. But she did have nice legs.

Lester had come out of his shell and was talking up a storm about growing up in Austin. Sarah Patterson, Fargo noticed, kept bringing up his father.

Bronack wasn't with them. Once Patterson learned he was their bodyguard, she'd insisted he eat with the hired help in the kitchen.

At the moment Dandy was saying, "We've traveled a considerable distance to see the bowie. I hope you won't mind if I ask how you came to possess it?"

"Not at all, sweetie. It was Charlie's grandfather's," Sarah said. "How he got it I don't know, although there was a rumor that he happened to be passing through San Antonio shortly after the Alamo fell and somehow got his hands on it."

"There was a lot of confusion back then as to what happened to their possessions after Santa Anna disposed of their bodies," Dandy said. "Some say the Mexican soldiers helped themselves. Others that their effects were buried with them or burned."

"Really?" Sarah sounded as if she couldn't possibly be less interested. "Charlie was fond of the knife. He had a great respect for Jim Bowie. He was always going on about that sandbar fight Bowie was in, and how Bowie cut a man's heartstrings."

"I would have liked to have met him," Dandy said.

Sarah shrugged. "I've heard tell that he ran slaves. Charlie said a lot of people did back then but you wouldn't catch me doing it."

Fargo glanced at her servants and had a thought he kept to himself.

"Charlie treated the knife as if it were priceless," Sarah related. "Every now and then he'd take it out and fondle it as if it were me." She laughed without mirth.

"I can't wait to see it."

Sarah sat back, touched her cloth napkin to her lips, and placed it in her lap. "I suppose you've been kept in suspense long enough." She clapped her hands at Miquel. "Fetch it for us, would you."

"*Si, Senora* Patterson."

Dandy fidgeted in her chair. "Aren't you excited, Les?" she asked her brother.

"I'm so worked up I can't stand it," Lester said dryly.

Miquel wasn't gone long. He returned bearing a polished oak case a foot and a half long and about five inches wide. Setting it in front of Sarah Patterson, he backed away.

"The blade that belonged to the legendary Jim Bowie," Sarah said, and slid it across to Dandy.

"Oh, my," Dandy said like a little girl given a present. "This is a moment I'll never forget."

"Me either," Lester said in his droll way.

"I thank you for letting me look at it first," Dandy said to Sarah.

"Who else? Your brother couldn't give a damn and handsome, there, can't keep his eyes off my legs." Sarah grinned at Fargo.

"Hell," Fargo said. He didn't realize he was that obvious.

"No need to be embarrassed about an appetite."

"Is that what you call it?" Fargo said.

"It's what I call it. Others call it true love or romance or nonsense like that. I wouldn't know true love if it bit me on the backside."

"Yet you've been married more than once, I hear," Lester threw in.

"What does marriage have to do with true love?"

Dandy wasn't paying attention to them. She was reverently running her hand over the oak case and now she tilted it to look at the bottom. "There aren't any markings to show who made this."

"Who cares about the case?" Sarah said. "It's the knife that counts."

Dandy drew it closer and delicately opened a tiny bronze clasp. She gripped both ends of the lid, took a deep breath, and slowly raised it.

Fargo saw her eyes widen. He couldn't see why; the lid blocked his view. When she sat there staring, he prompted her with, "Well?"

"Yes. Say something, consarn you," Lester said. "Don't keep me in suspense. Will we waste more of Father's money or not?"

"Waste?" Sarah Patterson said.

"Come see, both of you," Dandy said, beckoning.

Fargo came around the table on the right, Lester on the left.

"It can't be," Lester said.

Fargo had to admit the knife appeared authentic. It was old, for one thing. The hilt was well worn. He guessed the blade to be nine to ten inches long and half as wide as his palm. A guard between the blade and the hilt prevented the hand from slipping during a fight. But it was the blood that piqued his interest. Blotches marked the blade, from tip to guard, the red long since faded to a rust hue.

"It has to be a fake," Lester said.

"Are you suggesting that I'm trying to dupe you?" Sarah Patterson testily asked.

"My apologies," Lester said. "I should be more respectful of my elders."

"I'm commencing to dislike you, boy," Sarah said.

"What did I do?"

Dandy bent over the bowie and respectfully touched the hilt.

"It won't bite," Sarah said, laughing.

"That it might actually be the knife Jim Bowie wore at the Alamo . . ." Dandy said in amazement. "Who knows how many lives it's taken?"

"There's a little issue of the money," Sarah said.

"I'll make you an offer after I've examined it," Dandy said. "It could take a while."

"Take as long as you need." Sarah looked at Fargo, at a spot below his belt, and smirked. "Whatever will I do with myself while you're busy?"

"Let's eat so I can start," Dandy said.

The meal was an unusual mix of steak and potatoes and pinto beans and tacos. Fargo washed it down with two glasses of some of the best whiskey he'd ever tasted. When he pushed his plate back he was fit to burst.

Sarah Patterson didn't eat enough for a bird, which explained her figure. "Who wants dessert?"

"Not me," Dandy said. "I'd like to get started on the knife. Is there somewhere private, if you don't mind?"

"Why would I?" Sarah rejoined. "I hope you don't think I'd try to deceive you? To what end? I'm quite wealthy, thanks to my dear, departed husbands. I don't need your money. I merely expect our agreement to be honored." She smiled and crossed her legs. "To be frank, I don't know why I contacted your father. I happened to see the case one day on the stand where Charlie kept it, and remembered hearing that your father collects things from the Alamo. And here you are." She flicked a finger at the case. "It means nothing to me."

"But you're a Texan," Dandy said. "How can you say that?"

"I don't have much interest in the past," Sarah said. "I live for the present and take what joys I can while I'm alive. I could stare at that knife all day and not get the tingle I feel when I stare at you."

"At me?" Dandy said.

"I also get a tingle from men with lots of money," Sarah went on with a grin. "When I met Charlie Patterson and learned about his ranch and his bank account, I tingled all over."

Dandy appeared shocked. "Surely that wasn't the only reason you married him?"

"What other reason is there?"

"Love," Dandy said.

"You must not have heard me earlier. I don't believe in all that romantic nonsense," Sarah said, shaking her head in amusement. "It's hogwash."

"You didn't love any of your husbands? Not a single one?"

"I loved their money. Each was richer than the last.

Charlie had the most of all of them, and the most land, besides." Sarah cocked her head. "Don't look at me like that, my dear. He benefited, too. He had my company all those years. And I let him poke me whenever he wanted."

"I'd rather not hear that aspect," Dandy said.

"Why not? It's as much a part of life as breathing. We eat when we're hungry, we hop into bed when we're randy."

"Women don't get randy. Only men do."

Sarah laughed and winked at Fargo. "Listen to her, would you? She's a child."

"I am not," Dandy said, blushing.

Sarah gazed fondly at her. "Sweetheart, you can deny it all you want, but when you strip away the pretense, women like to do it as much as men. Sometimes more. I happen to love it more than anything, and with anyone who strikes my fancy."

"That's outrageous," Dandy said.

"I prefer to regard it as being honest with myself. Not many people can be. They don't have it in them. They'd rather pretend life is what it isn't."

"I'm not quite sure I understand."

"I wouldn't expect you to," Sarah said. "You're young yet. Give yourself time. A few more years and you'll see that there's no such thing as love."

"I firmly believe there is. Just as I suspect that deep down you really did care for Mr. Patterson."

"He treated me decent, I'll say that for him. I shouldn't speak ill of the dead, but when it came to frolicking under the sheets, he was about as exciting as a lump of clay."

"Mrs. Patterson!"

"The truth is the truth," Sarah said. "That's why I had to look elsewhere for my fun."

Dandy was shocked. "Wait. You're saying that you slept around while you were married?"

"I told you. I like it more than anything."

"Did your husband know?"

"Do I look stupid?" Sandy said tartly. "I did him the courtesy of being discreet."

They ate their dessert in silence.

When they were finished, Sarah rose and announced, "I'll have Miquel show you to your room, Miss Caventry, so you can examine the knife. My maid, Lupe, will escort your brother." She looked at Fargo. "I'll take care of you personally."

Fargo stared at her bosom and did some tingling of his own.

A flight of stairs with a mahogany rail brought them to the second floor. Sarah led Fargo to a room at the end.

"Here you go. As far from the others as you can be. One of us could scream and they wouldn't hear us."

"I try not to scream more than once a year," Fargo said.

Sarah pressed against him, her hands on hips. "If I don't scream at least once a night, I'm a grump the next day." She touched a painted fingernail to his chin and lightly traced his jaw to his ear.

Squeezing her bottom, Fargo said, "Keep that up and you'll be screaming yourself hoarse."

Sarah suddenly cupped him between his legs. "What do we have here?" she teased. "You get hard fast. How about if we put this to the use the Good Lord intended?"

10

Fargo rarely said no to a willing filly. There had been a few times but so few he could count them on one hand and have fingers left over.

An inviting smile and a pair of shapely thighs always brought out a hunger in him. He craved the female body like some folks craved pie or cake or opium.

Some would say it was all he ever thought about but that wasn't true. Sure, he had it on his mind a lot, but it wasn't his fault he had a pecker.

A lot of folks thought it was sinful to like to make love. He thought it was loco not to.

Those same folks claimed there wasn't any fooling around on the other side of the pearly gates. That once a person reached heaven, they had no interest in "that."

To Fargo, that would be sheer hell. He liked pearls, himself. The twin pearls at the tip of a woman's breasts and the tiny pearl between her thighs.

When he didn't answer right way, Sarah Patterson got the wrong idea.

"What's the matter? Don't tell me you're married or you're hankering after sweet Dandelion and don't want to spoil your chances?"

"I wouldn't let that stop me," Fargo said.

"A man after my own heart. Then why aren't you taking me into your room and ravishing me? Are you shy when it comes to females?"

"Shy as can be." That Fargo was able to say it with a straight face was remarkable. Poker-playing came in handy.

"Don't fret. Lovemaking is like riding a horse. Once you learn, you climb on and do it without having to think about it." Sarah caressed his chin and kissed him on the lips. "Leave everything to me. I'll show you how it's done."

"I could use some lessons."

"You've come to the right gal," Sarah said, and chortled. . "I know more than most females forget."

Fargo liked confident women. They were much less inhibited. The timid ones had to be coaxed into doing something as simple as touching tongues. Ones like Sarah would suck your tongue down their throat.

Sarah kissed his neck and his cheek while running her hand up his thigh. "Far be it for me to brag but I've yet to meet anyone who has made love as many times as I have." She paused. "How many times have you done it?"

Fargo made a show of trying to remember. "Five or six."

"Then you're in for the time of your life."

"Shouldn't we go in the room first?"

"Oh." Sarah opened the door and sashayed in like a whorehouse madam entering her private boudoir. "This is one of my special rooms."

"Special?" Fargo stepped over the threshold and stopped in astonishment.

The room was pink, like the outside of the house and the rest of buildings. Only the room was completely pink: pink walls, pink ceiling, pink carpet, a pink dresser and a pink chair, a pink quilt on the bed. Even the bedposts were pink.

"Let me guess what your favorite color is," Fargo said.

"It's blue."

Fargo stared at her.

"I'm female," Sarah said, and nothing more, as if that alone explained it.

"Women," Fargo muttered.

"We have our uses. But you haven't seen the best part." Sarah walked to a closet on the far wall. Opening it, she gestured with a flourish. "Take a gander, handsome. I'll put on whichever you like."

Fargo went over.

It was as long as the room and filled from end to end with clothes of all kinds. Dresses, some short and some long, all of them cut low at the cleavage. There were the fancy dresses rich women liked to wear and the plain dresses of, say, a farmer's wife. There was a riding habit, a maid's uniform, a cook's uniform. And of all things, a nun's habit. Every last garment was pink.

"Were you kicked in the head by a horse when you were little?" Fargo asked.

Sarah laughed. "You haven't seen anything yet." She moved along the row and selected one and held it out for him to see. It had a strip of fur along the collar and at the ends of the sleeves. It also had holes where the breasts would be and another, larger, cutaway triangle low down.

"God in heaven," Fargo said.

Sarah nodded at the bed. "Shuck your hardware and make yourself comfortable. I'll be right out." She grinned and moved to another door and disappeared.

Fargo unbuckled his gun belt and hung it over a bedpost. He took off his spurs and tugged out of his boots. Sitting on the end of the bed, he leaned back to wait.

In barely two minutes the door opened and in came Sarah, smiling seductively. She had changed,. The dress fit her so perfectly, it must be tailored. "Like what you see, big man?"

Fargo liked what he saw a lot.

Sarah's nipples poked from the holes, and her bush showed at the triangle. The hem hung an inch below her nether charms, and with each sway of a leg, she showed creamy thigh.

Fargo got a lump in his throat.

"I had to pay twice what most dresses cost for these," Sarah said. "The damn seamstress thought it was unseemly."

It was about the most perfect dress Fargo ever laid eyes on, and he said as much.

Sarah laughed and turned in a circle, showing off her body. "I knew you'd like it. I sensed the moment we met that we're kindred spirits."

"Oh, hell," Fargo said.

"All I mean," Sarah said, "is that you and I have something in common. Something that most folks are too sissified to admit."

"I don't like pink," Fargo said.

"Not that, silly goose," Sarah said, coming to the bed. "I mean we both like to screw."

Fargo had to admit she had him pegged.

"That you've only done it five or six times is no fault of yours," Sarah said. "It's just that most people are too scared or religious to put their bodies to the use God intended. Or else they're cold fish who'd rather collect coins or some shit."

"The mouth you have on you."

"You'll see it put to good use in a bit. But first." Sarah moved around to the side and crouched and pulled at a drawer under the bed. "Take a gander at these. They cost a pretty penny, too."

Fargo peered over, and was dumbfounded.

The drawer was filled with all kinds of things to use while frolicking under the sheets: whips, chains, handcuffs, a riding crop, several "ticklers," they were called, and polished wooden manhoods in several sizes and shapes.

"You use all of this?" Fargo marveled.

"Only when the real thing isn't available," Sarah said, "and it usually is."

"None of them are pink."

Sarah chuckled. "That would be overdoing it." She gestured. "Any you'd like us to use?"

Reaching out, Fargo grasped her wrist and pulled her to him. "The only toys we need," he said, placing a hand over a nipple, "are these"—and he placed her hand on his bulging pole—"and this."

Sarah's eyes became hooded with lust. "I like it natural as much as the next gal."

"You call that pickle collection natural?"

"I can't help it you were born with one attached to you and I have to make do." Sarah bent and rimmed his ear with the tip of her tongue. "How about we get to it?"

In no time they were naked.

Fargo had lied to her. He'd been with more than five or six women. He'd been with a *lot*. But never, anywhere, had he come across a female like Sarah Patterson. She didn't just make love to him. She *devoured* him. She was more aggressive than any woman he'd ever met. As aggressive as, say, a man. Sarah gave as good as she got, literally, and then went further.

She was all over him. Her lips, her hands, her tongue. She left no square inch untouched. She fondled, caressed, licked, bit.

She would do anything. Anything at all.

It was like making love to five women at once. Five women who had gone without for a year and were starved with desire.

Keeping up with her was a challenge. Where a lot of females would lie there like bumps on a log and not do much, Sarah was a bubbling volcano of carnal cravings. Her energy was boundless. So was her hunger. She exhausted *him*.

The first time they made love with him on top. The second time with her on top. Incredibly, she got him hard a third time, pulled him to the carpeted floor, got down on her hands and knees, and said, "Do me like I'm a mare and you're a stallion."

Fargo did the Ovaro proud.

Later, much later, they lay side by side on the pink carpet, gasping for breath.

"Not bad, handsome," Sarah said.

Fargo was stiff and sore in parts of his body he never realized could get stiff and sore doing *that*. He was caked with sweat and he'd swear that he'd pulled a muscle down low.

"Not bad at all."

"I've had better."

"Like hell you have," Sarah replied. "There's no one better than me."

"Modest, too," Fargo said.

"Why should a person be modest about something they're good at?"

The meal and the sex had made Fargo drowsy. He struggled to say awake, saying "And you are damn good, lady."

"Thank you, kind sir." Sarah chuckled and caressed his cheek. "It riles me, though, that I can't do it openly without people pointing their fingers and wagging their tongues."

"You want to do it right out in the street?"

"Would that I could," Sarah said, and sighed. "But in the city, any city, I'd be a scandal. There would be whispers behind my back, and I'd likely be brought up on charges of inciting indecency or some nonsense."

"If you wear that dress to the market you would be."

"I'm serious, damn it. Those who don't like to screw are always trying to control those of us who do." Sarah rolled onto her back. Her eyes closed and she said tiredly, "Why do you think I stay at the ranch when I could just as well move to a city and live in a mansion?" She answered her own question before he could. "Out here I have the privacy to do as I please."

"That's nice." It seemed to Fargo that she had sex on the brain, but who was he to talk?

"It's another reason I chose Charlie for my last husband," Sarah said. She was almost asleep and he barely heard her. "I knew once he died, I'd have the privacy I needed."

"Lucky you" Fargo said.

"I can make love to whoever I like whenever I like. It's sheer bliss."

Fargo was about under but he heard her next words, which were whispered, quite clearly.

"Hell, I can kill whoever I want, too."

11

It was the first thing Fargo thought of when he woke in the dead of night. He lay there listening to Sarah's heavy breathing and an occasional snore and wondered about her comment. The tale of her killing those *vaqueros* and the owner of the rancho might be true.

Closing his yes, he tried to get back to sleep but couldn't. He felt strangely invigorated. Maybe it was the lovemaking. He was also also hungry as hell.

Quietly rising, Fargo dressed. He strapped on his Colt, attached his spurs, donned his hat, and ambled out.

The ranch house was so quiet he heard the ticking of the grandfather clock in the parlor before he got there.

A lamp was on, and he was about to pass by on his way to the kitchen when he saw why. "Are you up late or up early?"

Dandelion Caventry was perched on a large sofa, her legs curled under her. To one side was the oak case containing the fabled bowie. On the other was a leather satchel that had been tied to their packhorse on the long ride there. She had a magnifying glass and was examining the blade. "I haven't been to bed yet."

Fargo went over. "Is it or isn't it?"

"It could be," Dandy said uncertainty. "It's old enough, and there are initials etched in the hilt, under the guard."

"Whose?"

"They read '*JB*.'"

"James Bowie?"

"That's what someone wants us to believe," Dandy said, placing the knife in her lap.

"But you don't?"

"There's no mention anywhere in anything ever written about Bowie that he carved his initials in his knife. But it's something a forger might do to try and convince people it's real."

"Ah," Fargo said.

"The thing is, the initials are old. They're faded and worn, as they would be if the knife is genuine."

"Ah," Fargo said again.

"Is that all you have to say? You're no help whatsoever."

"You're the expert at old things," Fargo said. "I read tracks and shoot people."

Dandy sat back and studied him. "That's not all you're good at. I hear you're quite the ladies' man."

"Who would say such a thing?" Fargo asked in mock shock.

"Just about everybody."

Fargo caught on quick. "You checked up on me before we left Austin?"

"I was curious what sort of man Father had hired," Dandy explained. "At first I thought it was his notion of a joke."

"You've lost me."

"I'm rather straitlaced about that sort of thing."

"What sort?"

"The sort I suspect you've indulged in with Sarah Patterson, the hussy." Dandy averted her gaze and smoothed her dress. "Anyway, I was surprised to learn that someone else came up with the idea of hiring you and suggested it to Father."

"Who?" Fargo asked in mild surprise.

"My darling brother."

Fargo's surprise became more than mild. "Why in hell would he want me along?"

"He told Father you were the best there is at what you do and could get us safely across Indian territory. But I suspect he had an ulterior motive."

Fargo waited. She'd get to the point eventually.

"Lester didn't want to hire you for your scouting skills. He wanted to hire you for your—how shall I put this?—bedroom skills."

"I still don't savvy."

"You've no doubt noticed that Lester and I don't see eye to eye on a lot of things? One of them is how Father spends his money. Another is *that*. He thinks I'm too rigid. That I need to loosen up, as he puts it. But what he's really hoping is that I'll do something that will make Father mad and he'll end up in Father's favor instead of me."

"What you're saying," Fargo translated, "is that he talked your pa into hiring me in the hope you'd let me poke you?"

Dandy nodded. "Then he would tell Father and Father would disown me."

"The little weasel."

"You don't know the half of it. Lester has tried again and again to discredit me in Father's eyes so he'll get all or most of the inheritance."

"Would your father do that to you?"

Dandy wearily rubbed her eyes. "I'd like to say he wouldn't, that he loves me too much, but he's very strict when it comes to *that*."

"You can call it what it is."

"I'm a lady, unlike our hostess. Who, from what I understand, has been to bed with everyone in south Texas and is now working on northern Mexico."

Fargo laughed. "Your claws are showing."

"She practically raped you at the supper table," Dandy said. "I'm surprised she didn't let you have your way right there on the table."

"I wouldn't mind having you for dessert."

Dandy's mouth fell. "You've just been to bed with her and you proposition me? My God, you're cocksure of yourself, aren't you?"

"That's one way of putting it."

Dandy realized what she had said, and blushed. "Well, thank you for your kind offer," she said sarcastically, "but no. My brother will have to come up with a better way of turning Father against me."

"If he can do it without teeth," Fargo said.

"How's that again?"

"I don't like being used."

Dandy straightened and reached out for his hand. "Please. Don't take him to task about it. It concerns my family and not you."

"I'm the one he wants to bed you. It damn well does concern me."

"It's nothing personal," Dandy said. "To Lester you're merely another pawn in the endless games he plays with other people."

"He can keep his teeth then," Fargo said.

Dandy brightened. "You're willing to forgive and forget?"

"Like hell," Fargo said. "I might break a few of his fingers instead."

"When some people talk like that, I can tell they're only letting off steam. They wouldn't really do it." Dandy paused. "With you, I have the sense you mean exactly what you say."

"You're not a bad judge of character. But your brother sure is."

Dandy placed her magnifying glass in the satchel and stood. "Do I have to beg?" she quietly asked.

"Hell," Fargo said.

"Don't hurt him. He can be a jackass but he's my brother." Dandy touched his cheek. "You can see why I'm willing to overlook what he does, can't you?"

"It's called 'stupid,'" Fargo said.

"It's called love," Dandy said testily. "I doubt you know much about it since apparently your idea of love is in your pants."

Fargo laughed.

"Damn you. You're supposed to get mad."

"What's that saying?" Fargo said. He pretended to think about it and snapped his fingers. "I don't get mad. I get even."

"If you hurt him I'll never speak to you again."

"I have a better idea," Fargo said. "For a walk in the moonlight, I won't lay a finger on the bastard."

"Did I just hear you correctly? You're trying to blackmail me into *that*?"

"Think of it as a trade."

"You're despicable."

"An hour of your time and your brother can go on picking his nose."

"Oh. Now I see. You're poking fun. You don't really want to make love to me."

Fargo let his gaze rove from her lips to her bosom to her legs. "Care to bet?"

"I never," Dandy said.

"Seems like a fair bargain to me."

"You can't treat a woman's virtue as if she's a horse you're bartering for."

"All I want is the walk. Whether you do more is up to you."

"It sounds to me as if you're trying to force me to do it against my will."

Fargo shook his head. "I've never forced a woman in my life." He grinned and added, "Never had to."

"No, of course not, as handsome as you are. Any woman in her right mind—" Dandy caught herself.

Fargo held out his hand. "How about it?"

"Now?"

"We're both up and the moon is out."

"Yes, I know but—" Dandy stopped again, flustered. "It's too sudden."

"I can wait while your head catches up to your ears."

She scowled. "You poke fun at people a lot, do you know that?"

"I wouldn't mind poking you."

"If we go on this walk, you won't try to have your way with me? You give me your word?"

"I won't try to have my way unless you take off your clothes and say, 'Ravish me.'"

"As if that would ever happen."

"Secretly you want to shed your clothes. I can tell."

Dandy laughed. "It sounds to me as if all your conquests have gone to your head. You're too full of yourself, by half."

"Let's find out." Fargo wagged his hand.

"Just to be clear. You'll leave my brother alone no matter what we do or don't do?"

"Honest Injun," Fargo said.

"Very well." Dandy coughed and took his hand. "I'll go for a walk with you. A short one," she amended.

The front door was bolted. Fargo slid the bolt and led Dandy out onto the porch. She stood at arm's length, plainly nervous.

The ranch buildings were dark. Stars sparkled in the heavens and a crescent moon was on its westward descent.

"The cool air feels nice," Dandy said. She stretched, accenting the swell of her breasts.

"Hussy," Fargo said.

"Are you referring to me or that woman you were with—?" Dandy stopped, her eyes widening in alarm.

Fargo started to turn just as a hard object gouged into his back and a raspy voice uttered a warning.

"So much as twitch and you're dead."

12

Out of the corner of his eye Fargo saw that there were two of them in store-bought clothes and boots and hats. One was holding a revolver on Dandy. The other had a six-gun jammed against him.

With surprising calm Dandy said, "What do you gentlemen want? As if I can't guess."

Fargo imagined she was thinking of the money she'd brought to pay Sarah Patterson.

"Jim Bowie's knife," the man behind him said. "Where is it?"

"And the case it's in," the other man said. "We want that too."

Fargo wondered if Dandy had caught on to the man's blunder.

"Answer me, damn you, or I put a hole in your friend, here, and we beat it out of you," the man behind him said.

"If you shoot him," Dandy said, "you'll have every cowboy on the Bar P down on your heads."

"Smart bitch, ain't you?" the other hard case said. To his partner he snapped, "Show her what we mean."

Fargo was unprepared for the blow to the back of his head. Pain exploded and his legs folded and he fell to his knees.

"Skye!" Dandy exclaimed.

"Shut the hell up."

Fargo heard a slap and a scuffle.

"Hold her good, Sully," the man who had slugged him with the revolver growled, "and let's see if I can't loosen her tongue."

"You can beat on me all you want," Dandy said defiantly. "I'll never tell you where the knife is."

"How about if I beat on your friend, here?"

The toe of a boot caught Fargo in the ribs and fresh pain throbbed.

"Stop hurting him."

"Where's the damn knife?" Sully demanded. "Your room? Somewhere else? Take me to it. and keep in mind that if I don't make it back out, Chester, here, will slit your friend's throat."

Fargo could barely think for the pounding in his head, and barely breathe for the throbbing in his side.

"Please, no," Dandy said, and gave in. "The knife is in the parlor down the hall."

"Lead the way. Chester, you know what to do with that hombre in buckskins."

"Sure do, Sully," Chester said.

Fargo struggled to regain his full senses. He knew that the moment Sully and Dandy disappeared inside, Chester was going to do him in.

"I won't try anything," Dandy said. "I promise."

"I believe you, gal," Sully said. "Now move your ass."

He must have shoved her because Fargo heard her stumble and say there was no need for that.

His vision was clearing. He turned his head enough to see Dandy going through the doorway and Sully holding a Smith & Wesson on her. The other one, Chester, a rake with a rat's face, was watching them.

Fighting the pain, Fargo whipped into motion. He swooped his right hand to his Colt and pivoted on his heels, thumbing back the hammer as he drew. Chester started to swing around and Fargo fanned a slug into his gut that jolted him back a step. Gamely, Chester sought to point his revolver and Fargo shot him again, square in the sternum.

Over at the door, Sully had spun and came charging back out. He banged off a shot that missed.

Fargo fired as Sully went to take aim, fired as Sully stumbled, fired as Sully pitched forward and the Smith & Wesson clattered to the porch.

Dandy was pressed against the jamb, a hand to her throat. "My word," she declared in horror. "You killed both of them."

"They would have killed us."

Sully was down, and dead. Chester, though, was still alive, his eyes pools of hate.

Fargo pointed the Colt. "Who sent you?"

Chester had to try twice to spit out, "Go to hell, you son of a bitch."

"You first," Fargo said, and stroked the trigger.

At the blast, Dandy cried, "No!" and dashed to his side. "You didn't have to do that."

"A man doesn't want his brains blown out," Fargo said, "he shouldn't pistol-whip and kick folks."

"An eye for an eye, a tooth for a tooth. Is that your outlook on life?"

"Works most of the time," Fargo said, touching a knot on the back of his head the size of a hen's egg.

Shouts had broken out, both in the house and over at the bunkhouse. Lights flared in windows.

Bronack was the first to reach the porch. Half-dressed, his pistol in his hand, he stared at the bodies and at Dandy and then at Fargo reloading the Colt and came to the wrong conclusion. "You were protecting her? This was mine to do."

"You were beddy-bye," Fargo said.

"Don't rub it in." Bronack tugged at his pants. "I'm sorry, Miss Caventry. I won't leave you alone again."

"It's hardly your fault," Dandy said. "You can't be with me twenty-four hours of the day."

A dozen or more cowboys were rushing from the bunkhouse, rifles and revolvers in evidence. Some were shirtless and shoeless and one was hatless.

Out of the ranch house came Miquel and Lupe and other servants, and then Consuelo in an ankle-length robe and slippers.

"Well, well," was all she said.

Sarah Patterson emerged last, looking flustered. She, too, wore a robe she'd hastily belted, revealing her considerable cleavage. "What the hell happened? I was so fast asleep, I was out to the world." She glared at Fargo as if it was his fault.

"Cockroaches," Fargo said. "They grow big in these parts."

The cowboys stopped at the foot of the steps except for a stocky slab of sinew who came onto the porch. "Are you all right, Mrs. Patterson?"

"I'm fine, Brazos," Sarah said. She nudged Sully with her foot and moved to Chester and did the same. "These aren't my men. I've never set eyes on them before." She beckoned to Brazos. "You're my foreman. Either of these coyotes familiar?"

Brazos was bronzed from the sun and had a shock of yellow hair. The way he looked at Sarah Patterson told Fargo that he did more than ramrod her outfit. "When I heard the shots I was worried plumb sick."

"I pay you to worry about my cattle." Sarah kicked Sully. "Do you recognize these two or not?"

Brazos squatted. "This one here, no," he said of Chester. "But that fella you kicked, I've seen him over to San Gabriel a few times, at the cantina."

"Is he a cowhand?"

"No, ma'am. I don't rightly know what he did for a living although I think I heard once that he was partial

75

to the shady side of the law. A little stealing. A little rustling."

"A little killing," Fargo said.

"They must have intended to rob me," Sarah said.

"They were after the bowie," Dandy informed her. "They jumped Skye and me when we stepped out to take the night air."

Sarah's eyebrows arched. "At this time of night?"

"I couldn't sleep," Dandy said, her cheeks coloring.

"Is that so?" Sarah turned to Fargo. "Don't you ever get enough?"

"Enough what, ma'am?" Brazos asked.

Shoes scuffed in the hall and out strolled Lester Caventry. He was in his nightshirt and his hair was mussed. Yawning, he rubbed his chin and said, "What's all the ruckus about? I was trying to sleep." He saw the bodies and his arm froze.

Sarah laughed. "You look scared, boy. Does death and blood bother you?"

"Nothing bothers me," Lester blustered.

Fargo said, "Friends of yours?"

"What? No." Lester jerked his arms down and glowered. "What makes you say a thing like that?"

"Cockroaches are like snakes," Fargo said. "They nest together."

"I resent that. I have no idea who these men are or what they were up to."

"They were after the bowie," Dandy said again.

"That stupid knife," Lester spat. "Look at the lives it's cost. There were how many bandits the other night? And now these two."

"There will be more," Fargo predicted.

Both Lester and Sarah Patterson looked at him sharply, and the latter said, "What makes you say that?"

"They didn't get what they were after and whoever put them up to it won't give up."

"Wait," Dandy said. "You're suggesting they worked for someone else? They weren't doing it on their own?"

"Posh," Sarah said. "Somehow they heard about the knife and how valuable it is and came to steal it."

Fargo called her bluff by asking, "How many people know you have it?"

"What is this knife you keep talkin' about?" Brazos asked.

Her jaw muscles twitching, Sarah pulled her robe tighter. "Forget about that. Have the men carry the bodies to the woodshed. We'll bury them in the morning."

"Do you want me to have some of the hands stand guard?"

"No, I do not. Do what the hell I tell you." Wheeling, Sarah stalked back in.

"What's gotten into her?" Brazos said to no one in particular.

"I'm sure I don't know, and don't care," Lester said, sounding bored. "Since all the excitement is over, if you'll excuse me, and even if you won't, a soft bed beckons."

Dandy was about to follow her brother but Fargo said her name and ushered her to the far end of the porch. "This makes twice now. You better start taking this seriously."

"You think I don't?"

"What I think," Fargo said, "is that you should keep Bronack close from now on. Carry your gun everywhere and be ready to use it."

"I didn't know you cared," she said with a mischievous smirk.

Fargo stared at the men he'd shot. "This makes three times someone has tried to blow out my wick. I aim to nose around and find out who put them up to it and return the favor."

"More of that eye for an eye." Dandy shook her head. "I wish you wouldn't. I wish you'd let the law handle it."

"There isn't any for hundreds of miles," Fargo reminded her.

"What if I beg you to let it drop?"

Fargo gave it to her straight. "There's not a snowball's chance in hell."

13

The next morning Fargo was up before everyone else except the cook. In the wilds he was used to rousing at the crack of dawn.

He dressed and strolled to the kitchen where a stout woman in an apron was making oatmeal and humming to herself.

"Any chance of coffee?" Fargo asked.

She bobbed her double chins at the stove. "I just put a pot on. It'll be ready in a few minutes. I'm Esmeralda, by the way."

"I'm—" Fargo said, and got no further.

"I know who you are," Esmeralda said without looking up from her stirring. "You're the gentleman who shot those two dead last night."

"They were out to kill me."

Esmeralda raised the big wooden spoon to her lips and tasted the oatmeal, and nodded. "No need to say why. I'm just the cook."

"Just?" Fargo said.

"I know my place," Esmeralda said. "Mrs. Patterson made it plain as plain can be that I'm to tend to the cooking and baking and not stick my big brown nose, as she called it, into matters that don't concern me."

"She did, did she?"

"Yes, sir," Esmeralda said. "Mrs. Patterson can't abide

an uppity staff. She gave a speech about that shortly after Mr. Patterson died."

"I take it you don't like her much."

"Don't be putting words in my mouth," Esmeralda said. "She's the lady of the house and I'm the cook. She's the boss, and I'm the cook. She tells me what to do and I do it because I'm the cook."

"Let me guess," Fargo said. "Her exact words."

"You're a good guesser," Esmeralda said, and sighed. "There are days when I miss Mr. Patterson awful fierce. He was a good man. A nice man. He always treated me like a friend and not just the cook."

"Ever wonder why he took up with her?"

Esmeralda set down the spoon and wiped her hands on her apron. "No need to wonder. She threw herself at him. Her with her female ways. Why, it wasn't but the third evening they went out together that she spent the entire night. Poor Mr. Patterson didn't stand a chance."

"Too bad he died."

"Now *that* I do wonder about," Esmeralda said. "He was healthy as could be. In all the years I cooked for him, I never saw him sick once." Esmeralda tilted her head and glared at the ceiling, but it wasn't the ceiling she was glaring at. "Then *she* came along. And Mr. Patterson started to have complaints. About how he'd ache in the mornings when he got up, and how he felt puny a lot, and how his heart would pound in his chest."

"You don't say." Fargo had never even considered that Sarah got her husband out of the way so she could take over the Bar P.

"Again, you didn't hear that from me," Esmeralda cautioned.

"I know. You're just the cook."

Esmeralda laughed. "Let me bring you that coffee. And a biscuit, too, to tide you over until breakfast."

"You're a sweetheart," Fargo said.

"What I am is sad," Esmeralda said, "that people like her get away with whatever they want and no one ever holds them to account." She opened her mouth to say more but suddenly stiffened and snatched up the wooden spoon and turned to the stove.

In walked the lordess of the manor. She had on a smart riding outfit with a small round hat, and was carrying a crop. "Look who else is up" was her idea of a greeting. "I thought I heard voices. What were you two talking about?"

"The weather," Fargo said.

"Is that all?" Sarah said. "I thought I caught a few words that suggested something else."

"Your ears were playing tricks."

"Could have been," Sarah said, but she didn't sound convinced. "In any event, I'm about to go for my morning ride. Care to accompany me?"

"I'm content right here," Fargo said. He was looking forward to a heaping portion of eggs with juicy bacon and buttered toast.

"Too bad. There's nothing like a ride to start the day."

"I know something."

Sarah chuckled.

"Will you be wanting your tea before or after your ride, Mrs. Patterson?" Esmeralda asked.

"Today it will be after. Miss Caventry is supposed to join me when I get back and give her opinion about the knife."

"What if she decides it wasn't Jim Bowie's?" Fargo wondered.

Sarah shrugged and said a strange thing. "It's a means to an end, nothing more. I won't be upset. I'll offer it to others who might be interested." She tapped her riding crop against her shoulder and swayed out.

Fargo had a thought. "The bowie knife, Esmeralda. Did Mr. Patterson ever mention it to you?"

"Not a word. I only heard about it when Miquel told me how you folks were coming to visit and I'd be cooking for more than usual."

Fargo accepted a steaming cup of coffee, and when the food was ready, ate as if there'd be no tomorrow. As he was dipping his last morsel of toast in the last bit of yolk, he remarked, "You're about the best cook ever. If I had a ranch, I'd hire you away from Mrs. Patterson."

"What a sweet thing to say." Esmeralda came to the table, checked that the doorway was empty, and bent. "You're a fine gentleman, Mr. Fargo. You treat me the same as Mr. Patterson did. So let me give you a word of advice."

"I'll all ears."

"Don't trust that woman as far as you can throw me. Never turn your back on her. And never, ever, eat or drink anything she wants you to."

Fargo pondered that as he strolled to the front of the house. He was on his way outside but he stopped at the parlor when he saw Dandy seated on the sofa, as before, with the knife case and her satchel. She was holding the knife and turning it over and over in her hands. "What's the verdict?"

Dandy adopted a pained expression. "I honestly can't decide."

"I thought you know about old things?"

"I can authenticate everything from a book to pottery. But this—" Dandy held it so that sunlight splashing in a window made the blade gleam. "If it's a fake, it's well thought out. They got hold of an old knife and somehow aged the initials they engraved. The blood spots are a nice touch, too."

"Then you're going to make her an offer?"

"I don't know. Something keeps nagging at me that it would be a mistake. I hardly slept a wink last night and I'm afraid I'm not thinking clearly."

"Take a break," Fargo suggested. "Go riding with me and save the knife for later."

"The air might clear my head, at that." Dandy placed the bowie in the polished case and closed it. "Mrs. Patterson went riding a while ago. Maybe we'll run into her."

"I'd rather step on a rattler."

"Oh-ho?" Dandy said, smiling as she rose and smoothed the green dress she had on. "Has your opinion of her changed?"

"Not a lick."

"But you and she—" Dandy stopped. "That is, I suspect you did. And surely you wouldn't do that if you didn't like her."

"Why not?"

Dandy was almost to the hallway and stopped as if she had run into a wall. "Am I hearing right? You would have carnal relations with a woman you didn't particularly care for?"

"Why not?" Fargo asked a second time.

"Because *that* is supposed to be special. You should only do it with someone you care for."

"Says who?"

"Most everyone," Dandy smugly declared.

"I reckon you've never heard of whorehouses."

Dandy had a knack for turning pink in the cheeks. "That's different. That's only—"

"Sex?" Fargo said when she wouldn't or couldn't.

"Yes." Dandy coughed. "What you're saying is that to you, having *that* with Sarah Patterson is no different than having *that* with a prostitute."

"Did you think it was true love?" Fargo asked, and laughed.

"No. Of course not. It's just—"

"Don't make more of it than there was," Fargo cut her off.

"Are you a man or a wild beast?" Dandy asked. "Animals do it that way. They do it just to do it. I prefer to believe we're better than that. That when a woman and a man make love, they do it out of affection."

"You did hear me mention whorehouses?"

"Stop bringing them up. Yes, I admit that a lot of people, male and female, are like rabbits in heat. It doesn't mean I have to be."

"You don't have it in you to be a whore," Fargo said.

"Thanks," Dandy said. "I think."

"All this jabber is hurting my head," Fargo said. "How about that ride?"

"Yes, please. My ears can only take so much."

"Your ears?"

"Whenever I talk to you, they feel as if they're burning. I've never met any man as frank about *that* as you are."

"On our ride I won't bring it up once."

"You promise?"

Fargo nodded. He'd do anything to get her away from the house. It might induce her to let down her hair, in more ways than one.

That early, the air was crisp and invigorating. Sparrows chirped in a rosebush. Over at the bunkhouse, cowboys were filing to the cookhouse for their breakfast. The blacksmith stoked a fire in his forge.

Near the house, Lupe was picking flowers. She smiled as they came down the steps.

"Everyone is so nice here," Dandy said.

"Not everyone," Fargo disagreed.

The stableman, an older cowhand with a limp, insisted on saddling their horses and bringing them out.

"Where to?" Dandy asked once they were mounted.

"The lady gets to pick."

Dandy rose in her stirrups, her dress clinging to her long

legs, and surveyed the countryside. "How about yonder?" she asked, pointing at a stand of trees about half a mile away.

"Wherever you want," Fargo said. "I put myself in your hands."

"Oh, my," Dandy said.

14

It was a pleasant ride. The cool of morning had yet to give way to the heat of summer. Dandy wasn't in any hurry and Fargo wasn't about to rush things.

This was grass and brush country, for the most part. Due to the lack of rainfall, the trees tended to be short and hardy. Prickly ash, bluewoods, Spanish daggers, hackberries and more thrived where northern trees would wither away.

The stand Dandy took them to covered less than an acre. The trees were far enough apart and Fargo and her had no trouble threading through them to a small clearing.

"Wouldn't it be nice to sit here a bit?" Dandy proposed.

It was fine by Fargo. Not that they or their horses needed the rest. They dismounted, and she moved off about twenty feet, bowed her head, and clasped her hands as if she was nervous.

"I have a confession to make."

Fargo played along; some women resented it when a man saw through them. "You do?"

"I didn't bring you out here for the exercise."

"Oh?" Fargo would let her get to it in her own way. She was less likely to balk.

"It's been gnawing at me. You and Sarah Patterson. We rode all the way here from Austin and you never once tried to have your way with me. Yet you poked her the very night you met her."

Fargo decided not to mention that it was more of a case of Sarah having her way with him.

"I like you, Skye. I like you a whole lot. You're about the handsomest man I've ever set eyes on. Those blue eyes, those shoulders." Dandy wouldn't raise her head. "You must have heard that a lot."

"Once or twice."

"Remember, I told you I couldn't sleep last night? It wasn't the bowie. It was the thought of you and her. And how much I wished it was me."

"I'm plumb shocked," Fargo said.

"It's just that I don't have a lot of experience," she went on as if she hadn't heard. "I'm awkward at it." She closed her eyes. "And I hate the notion of playing into my brother's hands."

"I'll never tell."

"Neither would I. But that doesn't ease me much. Maybe I'm a hussy at heart."

"Do you plan to bring Bronack here?"

"What? No." Dandy laughed. "Not in a million years."

"How about the Bar P foreman?"

"Brazos? Goodness gracious, I'd never give myself to a man—" Dandy stopped and her lovely eyes narrowed. "I see what you're doing. You're showing me I'm not a hussy."

Fargo walked over and placed his hands on her waist. He was encouraged when she didn't pull away. "Never in a million years," he quoted her.

Dandy started to laugh but stopped. Suddenly she turned and gripped his chin and drew his face to hers. Her kiss was clumsy—she missed his upper lip entirely—but her passion was undeniable. She tried to suck his lower lip into her mouth. After a minute she drew back. "How was that?"

"You were a bass and I was the worm."

"I kiss like a *fish*?"

"You kiss like someone who hasn't kissed a lot, but we can remedy that."

"How?"

Fargo cupped her right breast. At the contact Dandy arched her back and gasped. For a moment he thought she'd change her mind and bolt for her horse. Instead, she threw herself at him and fastened her mouth to his neck as if she were trying to suck his blood.

He reminded himself she was young. He reminded himself she was green as grass. He reminded himself of the curve of her breasts, to say nothing of the curves lower down.

"Why did you stop?"

Fargo wasn't aware he had. Dipping at the knees, he eased her down.

Dandy didn't resist. She did blush redder than ever, and when she kissed him, her mouth was on fire. When she pulled back she looked him in the eyes.

"Not a word to anyone. Ever."

"My lips are glued."

"God, I hope not," Dandy said, and fused hers to his. Her hands roved everywhere she could reach, rubbing, inciting. Grinding her nether mound against his hardening pole, she uttered a tiny moan. "I want you."

Inwardly, Fargo smiled. She'd hidden it well. But then, some women didn't like to come right out with *that*, as she liked to call it. They'd rather beat around the bush. They'd rather act as if they had no interest whatsoever until the moment came when they couldn't hold their hunger in any longer. And then they became every man's dream: a woman who would rip a man's clothes off to get what they wanted.

In Fargo's case, Dandy nearly did. She swatted his hat and undid his gun belt and dropped it and then tugged and twisted at his buckskin shirt in such haste, she got his arm caught in the sleeve. He disentangled, motioned for her to stand still, and stripped it off.

Dandy did something few women ever had. She swooped a mouth to *his* nipple while her fingernails dug into his ribs.

Damn, Fargo thought. He pried at the buttons on her dress and got enough undone to slide it over her shoulders. He kissed her ear, her neck, the swell of her globes. A sharp yank, and the dress was down around her waist. He had a chemise to deal with but nothing under it.

Her breasts were superb. Perfectly formed, swollen and ripe, their tips upturned and inviting. Her belly was flat. Below that—Fargo couldn't wait to find out. He pushed and tugged and her dress slid lower.

Dandelion Caventry, her name aside, was a feast for the eyes. Her legs were as fine as her breasts. Her lustrous mane of hair and the beauty of her face were icing on the cake.

Fargo would never have guessed to look at her since he couldn't see under her clothes but she was one of those rare females blessed with a body that other women dreamed about having.

Spreading the dress out on the ground, he laid her on it. She clung to his neck as he did, yearning in her gaze, near breathless with her wanting.

"God forgive me," she said.

"For wanting to make love?"

"For an urge I can't resist," Dandy said. "For throwing myself at you like this."

"Hell," Fargo said, and got back to it.

At the contact of his lips to her rigid nipple, Dandy gasped. As he swirled and lathered it with his tongue, she moaned.

He placed a hand on her inner thigh and caressed higher. Her skin was so soft, so smooth. And so hot.

Fargo lost himself in her body, from her hair to her toes, every square inch. He licked, he kissed, he rubbed, he kneaded. He made her bubble like a boiling pot. He stoked her desire into burning passion, and then, at the cusp of her need, he parted her nether lips with his finger and sheathed it in her hot, wet core.

Dandy cried out. Her nails sank into his shoulders and she thrust against him in abandon.

Fargo thought of Sarah Patterson; two women in twelve hours. At a whorehouse in Denver he'd once had three women in six hours. But he'd been drunk and couldn't hardly remember them.

Dandy mewed.

It was time.

Fargo penetrated her slowly until he was all the way in. She shivered and raked his chest and bit his arm.

Their rhythm came naturally. It was instinct, as old as the first man and the first woman.

It was a while before they reached the peak.

Then Dandy raised her face to the heavens. "Oh, Godddd," she cried, and gushed.

Fargo let himself go. The tide of release caught him and swept him along and he lost all track of time and everything else except the feel of it.

After, they lay panting, she on her back, he with his arm across her breasts.

"Thank you," Dandy said.

Fargo grunted.

"You were magnificent."

Fargo closed his eyes. He wouldn't mind a short nap to make up for the sleep he didn't have last night.

"I knew you cared for me. I could sense it."

Her words sank in and brought him out of himself. "All we did was make love."

"Wonderfully so," Dandy said, and snuggled against him. "I can see us doing this every night for the rest of our lives."

Fargo frowned. He hadn't seen this coming. It happened from time to time, though. Some women just naturally thought that when they gave their bodies to a man, they became joined at the hip. Permanently.

"You can ask Father for my hand. I'm sure he'll be agreeable once I explain how I feel."

"Where in hell did this come from?"

"It's the proper thing to do after a man has his way with a woman."

Reluctantly, Fargo opened his eyes and raised his head. "When you said not to tell anyone—"

"I don't want it to get out that we did it before we're man and wife."

"Dandy . . ."

"Don't worry. I won't ever bring up Sarah Patterson. You're forgiven."

Fargo drew back and studied her. "You're goddamn serious?"

"Why are you suddenly so mad?"

"Get it through your head. This was one time and one time only. I'm not marrying you, today or tomorrow or ever."

Her eyes moistened and her lower lip commenced to quiver. "I've given myself to you and you don't want me?"

"I don't want a ball and chain," Fargo said, and regretted it when she reacted as if he had socked her. "You're a great gal, but—"

"All I am to you is a body," Dandy said. "The stories are true. You like to poke and skedaddle."

"I'm lying here, aren't I?"

"Don't quibble," Dandy said, offended. "How could I have been so stupid? I mean no more to you than Patterson does."

"She means nothing to me."

Dandy winced and a tear trickled down her cheek. "All women are hussies to you, is that it?"

"Look—" Fargo began, and gave a start.

They were no longer alone.

Men with guns were slinking toward them from all four points of the compass.

15

The first time it had been Mexican bandits. The second time, gringos. This time it was half and half—two men in sombreros and two more wearing high-crowned hats and vests. Each held a pistol and was turning his head this way and that.

They'd seen the Ovaro and the sorrel but hadn't yet spotted Fargo and Dandy in the grass.

Buck-naked and unarmed, Fargo whispered in her ear, "Don't move a muscle. We have trouble."

To her credit, she didn't speak, didn't ask what the trouble was.

Twisting, Fargo snaked his hand to his gun belt and pulled it toward him.

The movement caught the eye of one of the men in sombreros, who swung toward them and raised his pistol.

Fargo was quicker. In a heartbeat he had the Colt out and cocked and sent a slug crashing into the would-be killer's chest. The boom of his shot was all the others needed to realize where he was, and their revolvers blasted.

Fargo rolled, fired at the man to the north, rolled again, fired at the man to the west. That left the bushwhacker to the east, who was behind him. Dandy cried a warning as a shot cracked and lead bit into the earth not an inch from his head. He banged off a shot of his own and saw the man arch onto the tips of his boots and dip into a pirouette.

Two of the three were down. The first man he'd put lead into had staggered against a tree and was trying to take aim.

Fargo had one pill left in the wheel; he had to make it count. He aimed and fired a fraction of a second before the man in the sombrero.

A hornet buzzed his ear even as the man's forehead acquired a bloody hole.

Quickly, Fargo snatched at cartridges in his gun belt and reloaded. He was worried one of them would get back up but none moved.

The stand was preternaturally quiet after the thunder of guns.

"Is it over?" Dandy whispered.

"Hush." Fargo finished reloading and rose.

Only one of the four was moving, weakly trying to raise his gun. Fargo stalked over to him, careful to keep an eye on the others.

"Bastard," the man hissed.

"No, you don't," Fargo said, and kicked the man's hand so the six-gun went sliding.

"Damn your hide."

"Who sent you?" Fargo said.

"As if I'll say after what you've done to me." The man shuddered and blood trickled from his nose. "I'm lung-shot, you bastard."

"Give my regards to hell," Fargo said.

The man quaked and groaned. "I never saw anyone so damn fast. They didn't tell us that."

"They?"

The man coughed and blood leaked from his mouth. "She'll never make it back. Not with that much money."

Fargo thought he understood. "You were out to rob the Caventry woman."

"Rob?" the man said, and uttered a gurgling laugh. "You don't know beans."

"I know you're dead," Fargo said, and shot him in the head. Then he went to each of them to make sure. The last, a Mexican, was breathing, if barely.

"Who hired you?" Fargo tried again.

"Su madre."

"Funny man," Fargo said.

"Usted es un hombre muerto."

"I um, am I?"

The man was fading yet he got out, *"Mas pistoleros se enviara."*

"Figured they will be," Fargo said. He pointed the Colt but lowered it again. There was no need.

A twig crunched and Fargo whirled, primed to shoot. "Damn it, girl. Are you trying to get yourself shot?"

"I figured it was safe," Dandy said, staring aghast at the bodies, her dress clasped in front of her. "How many more will be out to kill us? I wonder. And who is sending them?"

"They wouldn't say." Fargo strode to his buckskins. For all he knew there were more out there, and as a general rule he didn't like to swap lead bare-assed.

Dandy followed, holding the bottom of her dress up so she wouldn't trip over it. "Didn't you learn anything?"

"You might want to get dressed," Fargo advised as he grabbed his pants off the ground.

"Oh." Dandy gathered up her clothes and moved toward the trees.

"Where the hell are you going?"

"To do what you told me."

"Get dressed right there."

"With you watching?"

Fargo bit off a few choice words. "You do remember making love a few minutes ago?"

"So?"

"Nothing," Fargo said. "Go behind the trees. And if you get shot, don't blame me."

Dandy gnawed her lip and set to dressing where she stood. "I suppose that was silly, wasn't it?"

"Silly as hell," Fargo said.

"Shows how much you know about females," Dandy said archly. "Just because a woman has let a man see her naked doesn't mean she wants him to see her get dressed."

"That could only make sense to a female," Fargo said. He scanned the stand. So far their luck was holding.

Dandy had turned her back to him and was dressing in sharp movements.

"Nice ass," Fargo couldn't resist saying.

She didn't reply or even look at him.

Fargo finished first and prowled through the trees in ever wider circles. He was almost to the south end when he spied the four horses the killers had ridden. There was no sign of anyone else.

About to gather up the reins and lead the animals back, it occurred to him to rummage through their saddlebags. He was searching for a clue as to who hired them. All he found were the usual mix of clothes, tin cups, ammunition, and whatnot. He also found a letter and gave it a cursory glance. It was from a sister to her brother, wishing him the best in his "grand adventure in the West." It was dated two years ago.

Dandy was dressed and waiting. "Are we safe?"

"For the time being."

"It was foolish of them to attack us," Dandy said. "What did they think, that I'm carrying thousands of dollars around with me?"

Her comment gave Fargo food for thought as they rode back to the ranch house. Brazos, the foreman, was at the stable, and when he heard what had happened, he sent half a dozen punchers to scour the countryside.

"Any strangers you come across, bring them to me. If they won't come, bring them anyway."

"They give us too much trouble," a cowboy said, "we'll bring them belly down."

Fargo was about to ask if Sarah Patterson had made it back safely when he saw her on the porch.

Dandy didn't waste any time dismounting and walking off. She was still angry at him and her back was as stiff as a washboard. She went up the steps and inside without responding to something Sarah said.

Fargo unsaddled the Ovaro and placed it in a stall. When he came out, Sarah was still on the porch, in a rocking chair. He made straight for her. He'd come to a decision. The way he saw it, only one of two people could be behind the attacks. To find out which one, he needed to stir them up.

"What happened out there?" Sarah asked as he climbed the porch steps. "I asked your darling Miss Caventry why she looked so mad and she wouldn't answer me."

"We were bushwhacked," Fargo said.

"That would do it," Sarah said. "But I suspect something else has her drawers in a knot. I suspect that something is you."

"I must have missed the part where it's any of your business."

Sarah feigned shock. "Is that any way to talk to a lady after you've screwed her brains out?"

"There were four of them this time," Fargo informed her. "It could be that two were from south of the border."

"Could be?"

"Texas was part of Mexico before it was part of the United States." Fargo paused. "And your ranch straddles both."

"Go to hell," Sarah said. "I had nothing to do with any of these tries on your life."

"Someone does. And if it's you, you'll pay."

"I didn't take you for the blustering kind."

"Consider this your only warning," Fargo said, and walked off. He'd shaken one tree. Now to shake the other.

Lester didn't answer until the fifth knock. Cracking the door, he frowned and said, "What the hell do you want?"

"Nice day if it doesn't rain," Fargo said.

"I have no time for your nonsense. Go bother someone else."

Lester started to close the door and Fargo threw his shoulder against it, slamming it into Lester and knocking him back. Before Lester could recover, Fargo was inside.

"You could have hurt me doing that," Lester said, his small fists bunched.

"I'll only say this once. Leave your sister be."

Lester's mouth worked as if he were chewing tobacco. Finally he spat, "What the hell are you talking about?"

"Someone is hiring the gun hands who keep trying to spill our blood."

"And you blame me?"

"Why not?"

"They're after money. *Our* money," Lester stressed. "Haven't you been paying attention? Do you seriously think I want them to take money that belongs to me?"

Fargo stepped up to him.

Recoiling a step, Lester jutted his chin in defiance. "Do your worst."

"My worst," Fargo said, "would end with you not breathing."

Lester's Adam's apple bobbed.

"The next try on your sister's life, I'll come looking for you."

"You don't scare me," Lester said, although he sounded plenty afraid.

Wheeling, Fargo strode out. There, he'd done it. He'd provoked both of them. Now all he had to do was wait for it to bring a rain of hot lead down on his head and hope he survived.

16

The get-together was in the parlor at four in the afternoon.

They were all there when Fargo entered. He didn't bother taking a seat but leaned against a wall and folded his arms.

"Let's begin," Dandy said. She was on the settee with the oak case in her lap and the satchel at her feet.

Behind the settee stood Bronack, his hand on his revolver.

Lester had plopped into a chair and hooked one leg over an arm. He looked as bored as a human being could look and picked at his front teeth with a fingernail. He stopped picking for a few seconds to glare at Fargo.

Sarah Patterson had claimed the largest chair in the room. She gave Fargo the sort of smile a rattler might give a mouse it was about to swallow.

Dandy said, "I want to thank all of you for bearing with me. It's taken longer than I expected to come to a decision."

"Too long," Lester muttered.

Dandy ran her hand over the case lid. "It hasn't been easy. Not that I would ever impugn Mrs. Patterson's integrity by implying she would engage in fraud."

"I certainly hope not," Sarah said.

"It could well be that her husband's father was mistaken. That someone told him this is Jim Bowie's knife and he took it for granted it was true."

"My husband, rest his soul, never told a lie a day in his life," Sarah said. "Nor, I understand, did his father."

"Any cherry trees around here?" Lester asked.

"Keep it up, boy," Sarah said, "and I'll have some of my hands take you out and tie you to one."

"Please," Dandy said. "Let's stop spatting, shall we? We're all friends here."

Sarah snorted.

"Anyway," Dandy said, and opened the case, "to the point. I've examined the knife as thoroughly as I can. The metal, the workmanship, the style, its age, all indicate that it could well be Jim Bowie's blade."

"You'll buy it, then?" Sarah asked.

"Let me finish. My father left its purchase entirely up to me. At my complete discretion, was how he phrased it." Dandy took the knife out and held it in both hands so all of them could see it.

"This is a large bush you're talking around, dearie," Sarah remarked.

"I'm almost done." Dandy touched a spot of blood on the blade. "While everything indicates it might be the real article, part of me, my intuition, isn't so sure."

"Well, hell," Sarah said.

"But I can't let that stand in the way," Dandy said quickly. "If there's the slightest chance it's genuine, I have to do what common sense dictates."

"You're not saying what I think you're saying," Lester said.

"Yes, dear brother," Dandy addressed him. "It's better to have the knife and later find out it's fake than to not buy it now and later have it proven to be authentic. So, I've decided to bite the bullet and buy it."

Lester looked fit to spit nails but Sarah Patterson laughed merrily.

"How much is your father willing to pay?"

Dandy looked at her. "Ten thousand dollars."

"Be serious," Sarah scoffed. "We're talking about the weapon Jim Bowie used at the Alamo. It's priceless. I won't accept less than, say, one hundred thousand."

Dandy placed the knife in the case. "My father is a wealthy man but he's not an idiot. He won't pay that much unless the knife has been proven to be authentic beyond any shadow of a doubt. I'm willing to go as high as twenty thousand."

"You insult me, child," Sarah said. "I might be willing to sell it for as low as eighty."

"Thirty is the highest I can possibly offer."

"Sixty, then," Sarah bargained. "That's more than reasonable."

Dandy seemed to be mulling it over and finally shook her head. "I'm sorry. The very most I could pay you is fifty. And that's my final bid."

"Deal," Sarah said.

Fargo had a sense that she had been playing with Dandy and knew all along Dandy would never go much higher than that.

"Very well," Dandy said, and smiled. "As it turns out, I happen to have a bank draft for that very amount."

"What a coincidence," Sarah said.

Lester swung his leg to the floor and sat up. "Wait. Did I hear you right? A bank draft? You didn't bring money?"

"Not a dollar beyond our traveling expenses," Dandy said. "What, did you think I brought cash? Where did I carry it? In my bloomers?"

"I heard you tell Father—" Lester said, and stopped.

"You must have heard only part of our conversation," Dandy said.

Sarah piped up with, "I don't care what form the money is in so long as I'm paid."

"I'll sign the draft over to you right this minute," Dandy said, "and we can conclude our business and be on our way."

"So late in the day?" Sarah gazed at a window. "You wouldn't get far before nightfall. Why not spend another night and head out early in the morning?"

"I suppose that makes more sense," Dandy conceded. "Is it all right with you, Mr. Fargo?"

"Why wouldn't it be?" Fargo could do some nosing around and maybe find out who to thank for the attempts on his life.

Just then there was a loud pounding on the front door. Miquel hurried down the hall and muffled words were exchanged.

In a few moments the ranch foreman, Brazos, appeared, his hat in hand.

"Beggin' your pardon, ma'am."

"Don't stand there like a dunce," Sarah said. "Out with it."

"Thad Sumpter just rode in. He spotted riders on the Bar P."

"How many?"

"Thad says they were too far off to tell much but he reckons as how there were six or better," Brazos elaborated. "I had him roundin' up strays that drifted into the brush along the river, and he was on his way back and happened to look over his shoulder and there the riders were."

"Injuns?"

"He thinks no."

"Ask him how far off. And which direction they were headed."

"I already did, ma'am. He thought it could be five miles, give or take, and they were headin' east."

"I don't like it," Sarah said.

"Can't it just be someone crossing your ranch?" Dandy brought up.

"After all that's happened, why take chances?" Sarah said. "Besides, crossing my ranch to where? The main trail runs north and south."

"What's to the east?" Dandy asked.

"Easterners. And there are quicker ways to get there than crossing the Bar P." Sarah speared a finger at her foreman. "Corral everyone at the bunkhouse and go have a look-see. If you find them, demand to know who they are and what they're up to."

"If I take all the hands there won't be anyone to protect the house, and you," Brazos said.

"Don't argue. If there's six of them you'll need all the guns you can muster."

"Yes, ma'am."

Sarah surprised Fargo by turning to him. "How about you, big man? Why don't you tag along? Another *pistola* might come in handy."

Fargo's inclination was to say yes. But a feeling came over him that it was wiser to stay put. "I reckon not," he said.

Sarah didn't hide her disappointment. "After the hospitality I've shown you?" She scowled. "Very well. Why are you still standing there, Brazos?"

The foreman gave an awkward bow and clomped off.

"Let's conclude our business, dearie," Sarah said to Dandy. "Come upstairs and I'll sign whatever you need me to sign."

With Bronack in tow, they departed.

That left Lester, who wore his sulks like some people wore clothes. "All that money," he said to the air. "Damn the Alamo, anyhow."

"Davy Crockett just rolled over in his grave," Fargo said.

Lester scowled. "I forgot you were there. Pay no attention to me."

"I try not to."

"Hardy-har-har," Lester said, and departed in a huff.

Fargo went out to the porch and claimed the rocking chair. He'd seldom visited a ranch where there wasn't one, and this was a dandy. High-backed, with a soft cushion on the seat and arms wide enough for a coffee cup to sit on. It was as comfortable as a chair could be.

Presently, cowboys filed from the bunkhouse and in no time had their horses ready. At a shout from Brazos, they thundered after their quarry. A dust cloud rose and hung in the air long after they were out of sight.

With the punchers gone, only the blacksmith and the stableman were left. The ranch was silent save for the occasional clucking of the chickens and, in the distance, the infrequent lowing of cattle.

Not quite an hour had passed when the screen door squeaked and out came Dandy. Her shadow, Bronack, trailed after her and moved to the other end of the porch and leaned on the rail.

"Here you are," Dandy said. "I've been looking all over for you."

"Thought you were mad at me," Fargo said.

"I was miffed but I got over it." She roosted in the other chair. "It angered me that you don't seem to hold a high opinion of my gender."

"Like hell," Fargo said. "No man holds a higher one."

"You made it sound that if you were born female, you'd shoot yourself."

"Ever hear of a sense of humor?"

Dandy's lips curled in a self-conscious grin. "You're not the first person to tell me I take things too seriously."

"But you make love really nice," Fargo said.

"God," Dandy said, and laughed. She changed the subject with, "What are you doing out here, anyhow?"

"Waiting for the fireworks to commence."

"It's not the Fourth of July. What fireworks would these be?"

"The fireworks where people try to kill me," Fargo said.

17

Dandelion Caventry was gorgeous and smart as a whip. She used words most saloon doves hadn't ever heard. She had a lot going for her, yet any dove in any saloon anywhere had more common sense. "Why should someone try to harm us now that the purchase has been concluded?"

"What difference does that make?"

"Are you seriously suggesting those men that cowboy saw would attack the ranch house? With all the hands Sarah has?"

"The hands are gone."

"The riders don't know that."

"You can bet they're keeping an eye on the place," Fargo suspected, "and sure as hell do."

The screen door opened and out sashayed Sarah. "What are you two talking about, if I might ask?"

Dandy answered, "Skye, here, is worried we might be attacked."

"Preposterous," Sarah said.

"That's what I told him," Dandy agreed. "If you ask me, he's a worrywart."

Fargo had been scanning the horizon. "Brazos and your men road off to the southeast," he mentioned.

"Yes. So?" Sarah said.

Pointing to the north, Fargo said, "Who's raising that dust, then?"

Sarah and Dandy and Bronack all looked, and the body-guard swore.

It wasn't a lot but it was more than two or three riders would make and it grew with each passing second.

"Brazos said the riders were heading east," Sarah said. "That's the wrong direction."

"Unless they let themselves be seen so everyone would think they were heading east, and then they circled around to wait for your cowboys to leave."

"You make it sound like some grand plan," Sarah scoffed.

"It's been pretty well planned so far." Fargo stood. By now he could see stick horses and stick men.

Ten or more, was his guess.

Bronack came over. "Miss Caventry? We need to get you somewhere safe."

"It could be anyone, I tell you," Sarah said. "I do have visitors now and then."

"If Miquel and anyone else knows how to shoot," Fargo advised, "I'd arm them."

Bronack had hold of Dandy's elbow and was guiding her toward the door. "Please, ma'am. I can't protect you if you don't do as I say."

"I still think this is silly," Dandy objected, but she went in.

"She's not the only one," Sarah said.

Fargo opened the screen door. "After you."

"No thanks. I'll stay out here and see who they are. Go hide if you have to."

Hiding was the last thing on Fargo's mind. Hurrying to his room, he grabbed his Henry and cartridges from his saddlebags, and hastened back down. Working the lever, he moved to the screen door and crouched.

Sarah Patterson was in the rocking chair. If she was scared, it didn't show. She sat and rocked and watched the oncoming horsemen.

The stick figures had packed on pounds. There were nine, altogether, four wearing sombreros.

Fargo put his back to the wall so they wouldn't spot him.

Sarah got up and moved to the rail. Hands on her hips, she called out, "That's far enough!" when the riders were in earshot.

Slowing, they spread out and drew rein. An unkempt mass of gristle with a square face leaned on his saddle horn and showed a mouthful of yellow teeth.

"How-do, ma'am."

"Who are you and what are you doing on my ranch?" Sarah demanded.

The mass of gristle cocked his head as if she'd said something peculiar. "You're not very hospitable."

"You haven't answered my question."

The man looked at the house, at the windows. "My pards and me are on our way to Mexico. Could you spare some water for our horses?"

"There's a trough with a pump over by the stable," Sarah said. "You're welcome to help yourself."

"We're obliged, ma'am." The square-faced man nodded at the others and reined his chestnut around.

Sarah wheeled and came into the house. She saw Fargo crouched low, and laughed. "Look at you. I told you they were harmless."

"Keep going," Fargo said.

"No one tells me what to do in my own house."

"Keep going," Fargo said again, "or I'll carry you to the parlor and dump you there."

"You'd have to knock me out to do that," Sarah said defiantly.

Fargo patted the Henry's stock. "That's what this is for."

"Fine. Make a fool of yourself." Glowering, Sarah walked on.

The riders had climbed down and were taking turns watering their mounts. Their leader went from man to man, saying something.

Fargo was so intent on them, he didn't hear Sarah come up behind him. The first he knew she was there, a hand pushed on the screen door and she went back out. "What the hell?" he blurted.

Sarah moved to the steps. "You there," she called out. "Don't take all day."

"Ma'am?" the leader said.

"You heard me. Get it over with."

"You're awful pushy, ma'am." The leader looked at the others. "You heard the lady, boys. We're not doing it fast enough."

They started to unlimber pistols and several shucked rifles from saddle scabbards.

Sarah Patterson just stood there, staring.

Fargo leaned the Henry against the wall and was out the door and behind her in three bounds. He looped his left arm around her waist and hauled her back even as he slicked the Colt from its holster. Thumbing the hammer as he drew, he fired at the nearest rider. The crash of his Colt sent the man staggering.

"What the hell!" the leader bawled, resorting to a six-shooter of his own. "Look yonder! Kill that son of a bitch!"

Fargo made it through the doorway just as guns boomed. He heard the *thwack* of the slugs striking the wall and the doorframe. Shoving the Colt into his holster, he snatched up the Henry and continued to backpedal as fast as he could move.

"Let go of me," Sarah came to life. "I don't like being manhandled."

"How do you like being dead?" Fargo gave her a push down the hall. "Hunt cover. If you have a gun and know how to use it, I can use the help."

Sarah Patterson was simmering mad. She glared at him and balled her fists and her whole body shook. It was a wonder steam didn't come out of her ears as she barreled toward the kitchen saying, "I'll deal with you later."

Shouts had broken out, both outside and inside. From the vicinity of the blacksmith shop a rifle cracked. The pack of curly wolves responded with a volley and someone whooped, "We got him!"

Fargo retreated to the parlor and crouched where he could see the front door but anyone coming in wouldn't spot him. This was bad. He was greatly outnumbered, and Brazos and the rest of the punchers wouldn't return for hours. He had two women to think of, and the servants. As for Lester, he didn't give a good damn what happened to him.

Boots stomped on the porch. The next moment a sombrero-topped figure filled the doorway, his revolver out and cocked.

Fargo raised the Henry and fired twice into the serape. There was a squawk of surprise and pain, and the man folded to his knees with his forehead on the hall floor, his sombrero tilted half-off.

Fargo glanced at a side window. He didn't know what made him do it but he was glad he did. A grimy face was peering in, and a pistol was flourished.

Fargo dived flat as the window dissolved in a shower of shards. Lead bit into the floor almost at his elbow. He rolled, banged off a shot that missed but forced the man to duck, and then he was in the hallway.

He was temporarily safe from the shooter at the window but two more heads were poking in the front door. A rifle muzzle blossomed and spat flame.

Fargo heaved up and retreated, weaving even though there was hardly room for it. Another gun joined in and slivers flew from the walls on both sides. Somehow he made it to the next room.

More shots thundered. He heard a woman scream, and when the shooting stopped, risked a glance down the hall.

The maid, Lupe, lay in a sprawl, her limbs akimbo, scarlet forming under her.

Fargo jerked his head back before he was shot at. It hit him that the killers might be out to murder everyone in the house. They wouldn't want witnesses who could bring the law down on their heads.

Someone came running from the direction of the kitchen and a uniform-clad figure hurtled into the room with him.

"I am here to help, *senor*," Miquel said. He had a twin-barreled shotgun.

"Hold on to this," Fargo said, thrusting the Henry at him, "And give me that cannon." He took it before Miquel could think to stop him.

"Senor?"

"Stay put," Fargo said as he cocked both hammers.

"But I can shoot, *senor*. And there are many of them."

"Don't remind me." Fargo poked his head out again. The front doorway was empty. From the sound of things, the raiders were up to something. Shouts came from several directions.

"Senor!" Miquel cried, and pointed at a window.

Fargo whirled. One of the invaders was leveling a rifle. He cut loose from the hip, the right barrel only. He didn't know what the shotgun was loaded with but he found out. Buckshot blew the window to pieces and most of the man's face, besides.

"You did it, *senor*!" Miquel happily cried.

"Shut the hell up and get in a corner," Fargo commanded, crouching in case another raider tried the window trick.

Miquel drew himself up to his full height. "I am not a coward, *senor*. I will fight to defend the *rancho* and *Senora* Patterson."

"You and your mistress," Fargo said.

"Senor?"

"Get in the goddamned corner. You're less likely to take a slug."

Miquel was about to reply when a scream pierced the ranch house.

It sounded like Dandelion Caventry.

18

Fargo was in the hall before her scream died. It had come from the second floor. He reached the stairs without being shot at and went up them three at a stride. At the top he crouched.

From the other side of a closed door came the sounds of a scuffle.

He heard Dandy yell, and a thud and scrapes.

Heedless of the danger, Fargo threw himself at the door. It was open a crack, and swung in, spilling him to his knees.

Dandy was on her back on the floor, her hair in disarray. She appeared dazed and was bleeding from her mouth.

Two men were going out the window. One had the oak case, and even as Fargo set eyes on him, he slipped over the sill. The second man spun and brought a Spencer rifle to bear.

Fargo let him have the other barrel. The blast made his ears ring. At that range, the buckshot was like a cannon. It not only blew the man's chest apart, it lifted him off his feet and flung him like a rag doll out the window, taking most of the glass with him.

Fargo cast the shotgun aside and palmed his Colt. He took a step toward the window but stopped and went to Dandy. The blood was from a mashed lip. Her eyelids were fluttering, and when he put a hand on her arm, they snapped open in alarm and she clutched his wrist. "It's me," he said.

"Skye! They took the bowie. You have to stop them."

Careful not to show himself and invite a bullet from below, Fargo moved to the window. A hasty peek revealed a ladder had been propped against the house. Where in hell they got it from, he had no idea. He started to lean out and instantly drew back when metal gleamed at the front of the house.

There was a shot and a thwack in the window inches from where his head had been.

"Don't let them shoot you," Dandy said.

Swearing under his breath, Fargo darted past her and out into the hall.

"Where are you going?"

Fargo didn't bother to answer. He flew down the stairs, pausing at the bottom long enough to make sure the front doorway was still clear. He crossed to the parlor. Glass crunched under his boots as he sidled to the window he'd shot out. Below it lay the man whose face resembled shredded beef.

Fargo risked another look. No one was in sight.

Somewhere someone hollered and hooves drummed. Whoops and yips and shots filled the air.

Placing his hand on the sill, Fargo vaulted out. He sprinted to the front of the house and saw six surviving raiders galloping hell-bent to the west. One of the six, the man in the serape, reeled in the saddle.

Fargo did more swearing. He was tempted to go after them but it could wait. He moved around the porch.

Over near the blacksmith shop the blacksmith was sprawled facedown, a rifle near his hand. He wouldn't be shoeing any more horses.

The limping cowhand who oversaw the stable wouldn't be limping anymore, either.

The screen door did its usual squeaking and Miquel stuck his head out. "Are they gone, *senor*?"

"Afraid so," Fargo said.

Miquel stepped over the body in the doorway. "It was a massacre."

"Not even close." Fargo holstered the Colt and went in and reclaimed his Henry. "The shotgun is upstairs in Miss Caventry's room."

"You should have let me fight."

"Find your mistress," Fargo said. "I lost track of her in all the confusion."

"I don't need finding," Sarah Patterson declared as she emerged looking as mad as a wet hen. She walked to the rail, saw the bodies of the blacksmith and the stableman, and swore lustily, ending with, "Goddamn them to hell for this."

"You almost got shot yourself," Fargo reminded her. "Next time don't stand there gawking when men throw down on you."

"I wasn't gawking," Sarah said angrily. She bowed her head. "You try and you try."

"How's that?" Fargo said.

"Nothing," Sarah snapped. She stared at the receding dust cloud. "I want you to go after them."

"I aim to," Fargo said.

"Now. Right this minute."

"When I'm ready." Fargo turned to go in but she grabbed his arm.

"When I say now, I mean now."

Fargo shrugged loose. "First things first."

"What? You have to check on little miss innocent? I'll do that. I don't want those killers to get away."

"They won't," Fargo said. It wasn't brag. Six horses left a lot of tracks. And there wasn't a cloud in the sky so he didn't have to worry about rain washing them out.

"Damn it," Sarah fumed. "I'm not accustomed to not being obeyed."

"What do you want me to do, *Senora* Patterson?" Miquel asked.

"You might get your head out of your ass and see to Lupe's body. Or didn't you notice her lying dead in the hallway?"

"*Si,*" Miquel said contritely. "I will do it this moment."

"He's not much for brains," Sarah said to Fargo, "but he stays hard forever."

Fargo went in. He was almost to the stairs when Dandy appeared holding a washcloth to her bottom lip.

"Did they get away?"

"They think they did."

Dandy removed the cloth and frowned. "It won't stop bleeding."

"Give it a while," Fargo said.

"Have you seen Bronack?" Dandy said. "I asked him to bring me a glass of milk right before those terrible men broke in."

Fargo had forgotten about the bodyguard. He moved down the hall.

Miquel was draping a blanket over the dead maid. "So lovely a girl," he said, his eyes watering. "Lupe was a good friend."

The kitchen was quiet. Fargo found out why when he entered.

Esmeralda was by the stove, a hand to her throat, her eyes wide in dismay. At her feet lay Bronack, red spots on his chest showing where he had been hit multiple times. A broken glass and spilled milk lay near his outstretched hand.

"It was awful," Esmeralda said. "I'd just given him the milk when they came in the back door. He tried to draw but they already had their guns out. He didn't have a chance."

"Not him too," Dandy said softly, coming past Fargo. Kneeling, she stroked Bronack's brow. "He always treated me kindly."

The bodyguard, the maid, the blacksmith, the stableman. Fargo wondered how many more they would find. He was about to go to his room for his saddlebags when Dandy posed a question.

"Where's my brother?"

Fargo was embarrassed to admit that he'd forgotten about the pipsqueak, too. "Probably hiding under his bed."

"Lester might be a lot of things but he's not yellow."

"You sure we're talking about the same Lester?" Fargo pulled her to her feet. "Let's go check on him."

"My, you've gotten bossy," Dandy said.

"I get pissed when people try to kill me."

Lester's bedroom door was shut and Dandy tried the latch. "He must have it bolted."

Fargo pounded. When there was no answer, he stepped back to kick the door open, only to hear someone mumble and the bolt rasp.

Lester stuck his head out. His hair was disheveled, and he blinked and yawned and asked, "What did you wake me up for?"

"You've been sleeping?" Dandy said, incredulous.

Lester nodded and opened the door all the way. Smacking his lips, he scratched himself. "Why do you look as if you're about to lay an egg?"

"You've been *sleeping*?" Dandy grabbed him by the front of his shirt and shook him. "All the shooting and shouting and people have died and you didn't hear it?"

"Let go." Lester tried to pry her fingers off and couldn't. "You know how sound a sleeper I am. What did I miss?"

"The gun hands you hired paid the ranch a visit," Fargo said.

"That *I* hired? What in hell are you babbling about?"

Dandy let go of him. "My brother wouldn't do such a thing."

Fargo stepped up to Lester and he shrank against the wall.

"Good people died today. When I catch the bastard responsible, they're going to tell me who put them up to it. And if it *was* you—" He didn't finish. Wheeling, he strode off.

"Wait," Dandy called out. "Where are you going?"

Fargo didn't answer. He was still willing to bet his poke that her brother was behind the whole mess. Lester couldn't abide that their father was squandering their inheritance.

Sarah was waiting at the bottom of the stairs, impatiently tapping her foot. "At last," she said. "Every minute you waste they get farther away."

"Quit your bitching,." Fargo strode past her, thinking that was the end of it, but she caught up.

"I've about reached my limit with you. No one talks to me like that in my own house. Do you hear me?"

"Go bother someone else."

"Listen to me, you son of a bitch," Sarah said, and gripped his sleeve.

Fargo pushed her. Not hard, but enough that she thumped against the opposite wall and stood with her mouth hanging open. "You're not the only one who's reached their limit."

"You laid a hand on me!" Sarah declared in astonishment.

Fargo recollected their lovemaking. "Both hands," he said.

"And to think, I cottoned to you."

"And to think, I screwed you." Wheeling, Fargo kept going.

"Come back here. I'm not done with you," Sarah cried.

Fargo had no more time for her nonsense. There were bastards who needed killing and he was in the mood to oblige them.

19

It felt great to be in the saddle again. It felt even better to be shed of everyone at the ranch. They were grating on his nerves.

Fargo could stand only so much stupid. Lester, with his sulks. Sarah, with her high-and-mighty airs. Dandy, sweet Dandy, who hadn't woke up to the fact that the sheltered life she'd led wasn't the real world.

He put them all from his mind as he rode doggedly in pursuit of the raiders. Their tracks were plain enough. A ten-year-old could follow them.

The rolling gait of the Ovaro, the sun on his face, the warm breeze, were like a tonic. Gradually the unease he'd felt at the ranch faded and he was his old self again.

Fargo loved the wilds. They put him in a frame of mind nothing else did. Not even making love. It was hard to describe to those used to city life. Some might say it was peace of mind. He liked to think of it as becoming part of the wild, of being as men used to be before they became civilized, before they became timid and tame.

The tracks led west but only for a couple of miles. Then they turned north.

Evidently confident no one was after them, the killers had slowed.

Good, Fargo thought. He'd overtake them before the day was done, and there would be a reckoning.

Some would say he was taking the law into his own lands. But what law? The nearest tin star was hundreds of miles away.

Besides, Fargo preferred to stomp his own snakes, as the saying went.

The sun was well on its descent when Fargo caught sight of buzzards. They were wheeling in aerial circles as they gathered to feast.

By the time Fargo got there, the body was covered by feathered scavengers. The buzzards tore at it with their sharp beaks, tearing the flesh that was left from the man who had worn the serape. The wound in his chest had finally taken its toll and his companions had left him to rot.

Nice pards, Fargo thought. He circled so as not to disturb the carrion eaters. If any of the raiders were looking back, they might see the startled birds rise into the air and wonder why.

Now there were only five. But Fargo mustn't get cocky or he'd be feeding the buzzards, too.

Not long after he found the body, the trail turned east.

The killers, Fargo realized, had come in a half circle. By his estimation, he was now due north of the ranch.

Sunset arrived, spectacular splashes of bright colors that transformed the sky into a masterpiece of beauty no art could match.

Presently, twilight muted the colors to gray and after a while the gray became black.

Fargo reckoned he was close. Another minute, and a dancing finger of orange and red marked the location of their camp.

Fargo slowed. When he smelled the acrid scent of smoke, he drew rein. Sliding down, he let the reins dangle and slid the Henry from the scabbard. He also removed his spurs. He was leaving nothing to chance.

The mesquite was good cover. He crawled most of the

way, until he was near enough to see four of them seated around the fire, drinking coffee, and the fifth, the leader, pacing.

He didn't open fire. He waited, and listened. It could be they'd let slip the thing he was most anxious to know.

The leader stopped and stared to the south. "Where the hell is she?"

Fargo frowned. He'd been sure Lester was behind it. Apparently his hunch was wrong.

"The bitch will be here, Thorne," said a man at the fire. "You worry too much."

"I want the rest of the money we have coming," Thorne growled.

"Why should she try to cheat us?" another asked.

"We did as she wanted," said a third.

"I don't trust her," Thorne said.

"Hell," yet another said, and laughed. "You don't trust anyone."

Thorne resumed his pacing.

One of the men at the fire shifted and Fargo spotted the oak case. The man put his hand on it. "Do you reckon this is really his knife?"

"Jim Bowie's, you mean?" said the one next to him.

"Who else, jackass?"

"Enough," Thorne barked. He came over and stared at the case. "There's an hombre I'd like to have met. They say he'd fight at the drop of a hat, and he'd drop the hat."

"I hear tell he cut a fella's heartstrings in that sandbar duel."

The man with his hand on the case said, "They used knives a lot more back then instead of six-shooters. I wonder why?"

"Most guns were single-shot," Thorne said, "and not all that reliable. Six-shooters didn't come along until later."

"I never thought of that."

"That's why I lead this outfit and you don't," Thorne said.

A man in a sombrero remarked, "They say this Jim Bowie swindled your government."

"Swindled how?"

"He forged Spanish land grants and sold the land for *mucho dinero. Muy inteligente*, eh?"

"He wasn't so smart," another said. "He got himself trapped inside the Alamo, didn't he?"

"*Si.* And it made him famous forever."

"It made him dead," Thorne said, and turned as hooves drummed in the distance. "Hear that? About damn time. And she better have our money."

They fell silent.

The rider approached at a trot and stopped when the horse was just beyond the circle of firelight. All Fargo could see was a silhouette.

"What the hell are you waiting for?" Thorne called out. "Let's get this over with."

The rider gigged the animal. It was a woman, sure enough, wearing a capelike affair with a hood that covered her head and hid her face in shadow.

"You should have warned us, damn you," he said.

The woman didn't respond.

"You never said anything about that hellion in buckskins. If you had, I'd have asked for more money."

Reaching up, the woman pulled down the hood and shook her head to free her hair.

For one of the few times in his life, Fargo was genuinely shocked.

"Say something, damn you," Thorne snarled.

Consuelo placed her hands on her saddle horn. "We had an agreement, *senor.* I expect you to stick to its terms."

"Terms, hell," Thorne said. "I lost four men. Who the hell was that hombre, anyhow?"

"His name is Skye Fargo," Consuelo said. "He is the scout who brought the Caventrys."

"Goddamn you," Thorne growled. "You never told me his name."

"What difference does it make?"

"You stupid cow. I've heard of him. He's got grit to spare, and he's lightning with that smoke wagon of his." Thorne swore. "You and your great plan."

"It is not mine, as you well know," Consuelo said. "I do as I am told, the same as you."

Fargo had been about to make his presence known but he stayed put. He'd like to know who they were talking about.

"Let's get this over with. Do you have the money or not?"

"*Si.*" Consuelo shifted, reached behind her, and opened a saddlebag. She lifted out a leather pouch tied at the top.

Thorne took the pouch, set it on the ground, and opened it. Reaching in, he pulled out a fistful of coins and bills. "Well, now," he said, and smiled.

"It is all there," Consuelo said.

Thorne shoved the money back in and retied the pouch. "It better be or we'll pay the ranch another visit."

"That would be most unwise. The cowboys will be back soon."

"We can handle a bunch of cow nurses," Thorne boasted.

"Like you handled *Senor* Fargo, eh?"

"Go to hell."

"I will go to the ranch," Consuelo said, and held out her hand toward the oak case, "and take that with me."

Thorne gestured, and the man sitting next to it brought the case over. Passing it up to her, Thorne said, "You take a big chance coming out here by your lonesome. What if you ran into Comanches?"

"I am armed, *senor.*"

"So? What chance do you reckon you'd have? Why not light and stay the night with us and head back at daybreak?"

"Ah. So that is your purpose," Consuelo said. "No, thank you."

Thorne placed a hand on her leg. "I can pay. From my share of the money. And some of the others might like a poke, too."

"No, I said."

"Give me one good reason," Thorne said.

"How can I put this?" Consuelo smiled. "I would rather spend the night in a pen with pigs than spend the night with any of you."

"You little bitch," Thorne said.

Some of the men swore at her.

"Please, *senor,*" Consuelo said. "Why must you spoil it? Our business is concluded. I will be on my way."

"I should make you stay," Thorne said, "and then not pay you to teach you a lesson."

"I will not be threatened, *senor.*"

Leering, Thorne slid his hand higher. "Yes, indeedy. I reckon that's exactly what I'll do. Climb on down and let's have some fun."

"For the last time, *Senor* Thorne, I am leaving," Consuelo said coldly. "Take your hand off me."

Thorne laughed and reached up to pull her from the saddle.

Consuelo raised a hand as if to slap him.

That was when Fargo started to rise, and froze. A horse had whinnied. Not hers, an outlaw mount, tied in a string not far from the fire

The wind had shifted and was blowing from Fargo to them, and the animal had caught his scent.

Thorne spun. "Somethin's out there."

"Or someone," another man said.

All of them rose and drew pistols and peered hard into the night.

"Let's find out who or what, *amigo*," a man in a sombrero said to another.

The pair stalked toward where Fargo lay.

20

Fargo was furious at himself. He'd made a greenhorn mistake. He knew to pay attention to the horses and the wind. He was flat on the ground and well hid but if they came close enough they'd spot him. He didn't dare move the Henry to take aim or it might reflect the firelight and give him away.

"Anything?" Thorne bellowed.

"*Todavio,* no, amigo," the man in the sombrero said. "*Deja de gritar.*"

"Speak American, you damn yack," Thorne said. "I know your lingo but not that good."

Peering through the mesquite, Fargo tensed. The two killers were so close he could hear one of them taking quick, nervous breaths.

"I hope it's not Injuns," the nervous one whispered. "Apaches or Comanches, it makes no never mind. They're both bad medicine."

"Be quiet," the Mexican said.

"I lost my grandpa to Injuns. The Modocs. He got the gold fever back in 'forty-nine and went to California to strike it rich but all he got was caught and skinned alive and his throat slit."

"If you do not shut up, I will slit yours."

The nervous one stopped talking.

They advanced a few more steps and stopped.

Fargo stayed motionless. They were looking over him, not down.

"Don't take all night," Thorne hollered.

"Idiota," the Mexican spat.

"Don't let him hear you say that," the nervous one said.

Fargo waited for them to turn and go back. Should he have to shoot, the rest would hunt cover, and he'd like them in the open when he made his move.

"I reckon it was nothin'," the nervous man said.

"Si."

At last Fargo got his wish. They turned to go. He smiled, thinking the worst was over, when something crawled onto his left hand. Instinctively, he went to jerk his hand away. But the movement might alert the two outlaws.

Whatever the thing was, it scuttled onto his knuckles. He could make out a small dark shape, nothing more. It was too heavy to be a spider and had too many legs to be a lizard. That left one thing.

Scorpion. Some were abroad at night rather than in the day. Some were venomous, and their sting could knock a man out—or kill him.

The thing's tiny feet pinched his skin as it moved from his knuckles to the back of his hand. He could just barely make out its tail and stinger, arced over its body.

The Mexican and the other one were halfway to the fire. The Mexican glanced over his shoulder, and stopped.

"What?" the other one said.

"Something," the Mexican said. "In the dark I cannot be sure."

Fargo felt the scorpion crawl onto his sleeve. He was going to send it flying with a sweep of his arm but the Mexican took a step back.

Fargo imagined the scorpion crawling higher, imagined it reaching his neck. His skin prickled with goose bumps.

"What *is* that?" the Mexican said, and came toward him.

"Hope it's not an Injun," the other said.

Fargo strained his eyes until they hurt. He looked from his sleeve to the Mexican and back again.

The scorpion was at his elbow.

The Mexican was eight feet way.

The scorpion climbed past his elbow.

The Mexican paused, uncertain. "Maybe I am mistaken."

Thorne yelled, "What the hell is taking so long? Is something out there or not?"

Fargo couldn't see the scorpion. Had it crawled around his arm? Had it fallen off?

"Damn you, Carlos," Thorne shouted. "Answer me. Or do I have to come over there?"

"Fool," Carlos muttered, and turned to return to the fire.

Something touched Fargo's neck. He reacted without thinking, swatting at it and rolling. Carlos heard him and spun and a pistol flamed in the night. Fargo fired, worked the Henry's lever, fired a second time. Carlos tottered but he was tough and his pistol barked a second time, too.

Fargo continued to roll. He hoped to God the scorpion was off him because he couldn't stop to check. Carlos was shooting and the nervous one was shooting, and how they missed him, he'd never know. He shot Carlos in the head, swiveled, shot the nervous one in the face.

The rest were scattering, just as he knew they would.

Consuelo had reined around and was jabbing her heels.

On elbows and knees, Fargo scrambled toward cover. Changing position saved him; leaden bees swarmed the spot where he'd just been.

A small boulder offered haven.

Fargo hugged the earth until the fusillade stopped. It had all gone to hell. Now he had to hunt them. Just as they were hunting him.

Consuelo's hoofbeats were rapidly fading.

Fargo leaned the Henry against the boulder and palmed

his Colt. He snaked from the boulder to a cactus and from the cactus into a dry wash.

The desert was silent save for the crackling of the fire.

Removing his hat, Fargo sat it next to him, then eased high enough to see over the rim. Nothing moved.

They were no doubt doing the same as he was.

Fargo could be as patient as an Apache when he had to be. Only his eyes moved, darting here and there, seeking movement or a shape where there shouldn't be one.

In the darkness beyond the fire, someone cleared his throat.

"Can you hear me, mister?" Thorne shouted.

To say Fargo was surprised was putting it mildly. He didn't answer. He wouldn't make the same mistake Thorne was making.

"I have a proposition for you."

Fargo didn't reply.

"No one else has to die. This isn't about you and us. It's not personal."

The hell it isn't, Fargo thought.

"It's about the knife and we don't have it. That gal took it with her."

Fargo wondered what Consuelo's part was in all of this. Yet another question he aimed to have answered.

"Why swap lead if we don't have to? Think about it and you'll see I'm right."

Fargo wondered why Thorne kept on shouting. It was stupid. It let him know where Thorne was. Maybe Thorne thought he was stupid enough to answer so they would know where he was. He started crawling toward the spot where the shouts came from.

"This is a job to us, nothing more," Thorne went on. "You can ride away and there'll be no hard feelings."

Too late for that, Fargo reflected. He'd liked Bronack, and none of those others had deserved to die, either.

"What does it matter to you that we attacked that ranch? It's not yours."

Keep talking, Fargo thought. He was low to the ground, moving in slow motion so it wouldn't give him away.

"Just say the word and this is over. Me and my boys will light a shuck and you'll never see us again."

Fargo was near enough that he should be able to see some sign. He rose a little higher.

"You ask me," Thorne yelled, "a man can't let his feelings mix in or he'll make mistakes, and mistakes make us dead."

It was then Fargo realized that *he* was making a mistake. That he'd let Thorne lure him in with the sound of his voice. And that he had no idea where the other two were.

Even as he dropped flat, guns roared on either side of him. The whine of lead told him how close he'd come. He snapped a shot at a firefly on his right, snapped another at a firefly on his left.

Scrabbling backward, he got out of there. More shots, from Thorne's vicinity, nearly snuffed his wick.

Fargo had been careless. He took these men for run-of-the-mill and they were as sharp as tacks.

A shape closed, a rifle spanged.

Fargo felt a tug on his sleeve. He returned fire, once, twice, three times, and the shape vanished. He heard no outcry, no thrashing, so he figured he'd missed.

Heaving up, Fargo ran. They had him hemmed. To make a fight of it invited a permanent dirt nap.

Thorne had stopped shouting.

Fargo covered nearly fifty yards, and hunkered. His blood was racing and he was sweating profusely. It had been a close thing.

He thought of Consuelo. He wanted to catch up to her before she reached the ranch. He wouldn't if he stayed and fought it out.

A minute went by. More.

Fargo made for the Ovaro. He needed answers and Consuelo had them. He would go after Thorne later. He came to the boulder where he'd left the Henry and went on.

Something, a sixth sense, warned him to stop. He crouched with the Henry in one hand and the Colt in the other.

Something was moving. Something or someone. They would pass him twenty feet out.

Fargo bent so his chest practically touched the ground. Quietly setting the Henry down, he trained his Colt on the slinking figure.

The same sense flared again, a feeling that while he was focused on the man in front of him, another was creeping up on him.

Fargo shifted to look behind him. He wasn't halfway around when a blow to the head pitched him to his side.

"We have him," someone whooped.

Fargo struggled to raise the Colt but a boot stomped on his wrist, pinning his arm.

"No, you don't."

With his other hand Fargo grabbed for the Henry, only to have that arm pinned, too.

"Damn, he's a scrapper. He never gives up."

Someone else said, "He shouldn't have come after us. Some folks don't know when to leave well enough alone."

"So much for the great scout."

Fargo tried to wrench free but his consciousness was slipping into a black well. He barely felt the Colt being torn from his grasp.

"He doesn't look so great now," were the last words he heard.

21

Fargo came awake slowly. His head hurt and his throat was painfully dry. He smelled smoke, and coffee. He was on his left side. He tried to move his arms and couldn't; his wrists were bound. He tried the same with his legs; his ankles were tied.

"He's comin' around, Thorne."

"I've got eyes," Thorne growled. "And you might as well open yours, mister. It won't do you no good pretendin'."

Fargo blinked in the glare of the sun. By its position in the sky, it was the middle of the morning.

Thorne was across the fire, a tin cup in his hands. A swarthy Mexican and a pale kid flanked him. All three gave him flat, cold stares.

"I'm still breathing?" Fargo said in some surprise.

A humorless smile creased Thorne's mouth. "I could have splattered your brains but that would be the easy way."

"Ah," Fargo said.

"You have a lot to answer for," Thorne said. "Six of my men are dead because of you."

The pale kid produced a folding knife and opened it. "Let me carve on him. I'll whittle him a piece at a time."

"What you'll do, Charlie, is shut the hell up," Thorne said.

"I, too, want this gringo to suffer," the Mexican said. "He killed Carlos, and Carlos was the best *amigo* I ever had."

"He'll suffer, all right, Esteban," Thorne said. "He'll wish to die before we're done."

Ignoring the pounding in his head, Fargo asked, "Who hired you?"

"We're about to make you bleed and *that's* all you're interested in?"

"It would be good to know why I'm bleeding," Fargo said.

"I just told you," Thorne said. "Six men I could depend on are dead because of you."

"It was supposed to be nine."

"Glad we could disappoint you," Thorne said. He held out a hand to the pale kid. "Charlie, give me that clasp knife of yours."

"What for? It's mine."

"Are you sassin' me, boy?"

Reluctantly, Charlie set the knife in Thorne's palm. "I better get it back."

Thorne set the knife down with the tip of the blade in the fire. "We want it good and hot," he said to Fargo.

"You should let me do it," Esteban said. "I once rode with a breed who was half-Apache. He taught me things."

"I'll teach you things, too," Thorne said.

"Who paid you the money Consuelo gave you?" Fargo tried again.

"You saw that?"

"Why did someone have you steal the bowie only to give it back?" Fargo tried anew.

"Questions, questions," Thorne said. "But you don't know what in hell you're talkin' about. You're throwin' eggs at the wall and hopin' one sticks."

"You can't blame me for trying."

"I reckon not. I'd likely want to know, too, if I was in your boots." Thorne moved the clasp knife so more of the blade was in the fire.

"Tell me, gringo," Esteban said. "The other knife, the

one in the case, is it really the knife of the great Jim Bowie?"

"It might be."

"He was a man to admire, that one," Esteban said. "They say he was fearless. And he very much loved my land and my people."

"He loved them so much," Thorne said sarcastically, "he fought to be free of Mexico."

"He married the daughter of the vice-governor," Esteban said, "and they say he wept when she died of fever."

"*They* say a lot of things," Thorne said. "Me, I don't care. He's dead and gone. Fifty years from now no one will remember who he was."

"They'll always remember the Alamo," Charlie said.

"For a while," Thorne said. "Texans longer than most. But no one remembers anything forever."

"You think you know it all but you don't," Charlie said.

"I know people make a fuss over things that don't matter, just like you're making a fuss over who the hell remembers the Alamo."

Fargo had recovered enough to test his bounds. The ropes were tight. He could feel the Arkansas toothpick snug in its sheath strapped to his ankle but getting to it was another matter.

"And don't think I'm picking on your precious Jim Bowie," Thorne was saying. "George Washington. Thomas Jefferson. They're nothin' to me but dead men."

"I kind of like George," Charlie said. "He was honest through and through."

"Simpleton," Thorne said. He picked up the clasp knife and examined the tip. "Not quite hot enough yet." He put it to the fire again. "It needs to glow red."

"Where do you go from here?" Fargo asked.

"What's it to you?" Thorne rejoined. "You'll be dead when we ride out."

"I'm curious."

"You're damned peculiar, is what you are," Thorne said. "But me, I'm heading for Denver. It has more whores than New Orleans and some of the best sippin' whiskey anywhere."

"I wouldn't mind some red-eye myself," Fargo mentioned.

"I've got a little left in my flask," Thorne said. "But you ain't gettin' any."

"We could give him some as a last request," Charlie said. "That's what the law does when they're fixin' to execute somebody."

"Do I look like the law?" Thorne said.

"I hate it when you get in one of your moods," Charlie said. "All you do is bitch."

Thorne snarled and cuffed Charlie across the face, sending him sprawling. "That's enough out of you, you peckerwood."

Charlie scrambled into a crouch, his hand stabbing for his pistol.

"No." Esteban grabbed the younger man's wrist. "You are not fast enough. He would kill you."

Charlie was livid. "He shouldn't ought to have done that!"

"Don't overstep yourself, boy," Thorne warned.

Who knew what might have happened next if someone hadn't said pleasantly, "The three of you squabble like children."

The killers jumped up, and Fargo twisted his head.

Consuelo had gotten within twenty feet of the fire without being seen or heard. She was leading her horse by the reins, and her hood was down.

"What the hell?" Thorne said. "You're supposed to be back at the ranch by now."

"I had unfinished business," Consuelo replied. She looked at Fargo as she said it.

"What more is there?" Thorne said. "We have our money and you have the damn knife."

"I would like to talk about that," Consuelo said, "if you will permit me. I could use a cup of coffee first. It was a long night and I did not get any sleep."

Thorne motioned at the pot. "Help yourself, lady. There's plenty left."

Consuelo's blouse and skirt were covered with dust, and she swiped at them as she came to the fire. She was about to sit when she said, "I almost forgot. *Un momento*." She returned to her horse and brought her saddlebags back with her.

"What do you need in there?" Thorne asked.

"Womanly things," Consuelo answered with a smile. She set the saddlebags down. One flap was open, and the oak case jutted out. She opened the other flap and took out a tin cup. "For my coffee, *por favor*."

"Permíteme, senorita," Esteban said. He picked up the pot and filled her cup. *"Suficiente?"*

"Si," Consuelo said. She drank and sighed and fluffed at her hair.

"So what do you want to talk about?" Thorne asked. "It must be important for you to come all the way back."

"I want to talk about opportunity," Consuelo said. "Sometimes it is right in front of us and we don't see it."

"Opportunity to do what, exactly?"

"Whatever we wish. You, for example, had an opportunity to make a very great deal of money by raiding Mrs. Patterson's ranch."

"We earned it," Thorne said. "Some of our pards didn't make it out." He glared at Fargo.

"Si. But you knew the risk, yes? It was part of why you were paid so much."

"What's your point?"

"Opportunity for one can be opportunity for another," Consuelo said. "I was halfway to the rancho when I realized that and turned around."

"Do women *ever* get to the point?" Thorne grumbled.

"*Lo siento*. Be patient. I will get to it in a minute." Consuelo drank more coffee and did more fluffing.

It struck Fargo that she was stalling. Why, he had no idea.

"Take me, for instance," Consuelo resumed. "I am a *puta*. I have been one since I was sixteen, and I accept what I am."

Thorne yawned.

"I never gave much thought to being something other than a whore. Why should I? The opportunity to change my life never came along."

"God Almighty, woman," Thorne said. "Talk us to death, why don't you?"

"Let her speak," Esteban said. "I, for one, would like to hear what she has to say."

"Me too," Charlie said.

"Idiots," Thorne said.

"My point, *senor*," Consuelo said, "is that sometimes we are so used to our lives that we don't see opportunity when it is right in front of us."

"You rode all the way back to tell us that?"

"No. I rode back because I had missed an opportunity. You see, I have long desired to live elsewhere. I was raised along the border but the border isn't the world."

"It's not the moon, either," Thorne said. "Jesus, woman."

"Have you ever heard of San Francisco?"

"Who hasn't?"

"There are many people of Spanish descent, and the climate is mild. You don't roast in the summer, and there is the ocean."

"You like it so much, take a stage or book passage on the first ship that goes there."

Consuelo nodded. "I intend to, *senor*. But tickets cost money. And, too, how would I live when I got there?"

"You're a whore, for God's sake. Sell yourself like you

have been doin'. People pay for it there the same as anywhere. Stupid cow."

"Ser amable con ella," Esteban said.

"Oh, hell," Thorne growled. "I *am* being nice."

"That was sweet of you, Esteban," Consuelo said. "You,
at least, know how to treat a lady."

"Gracias, senorita."

"But *Senor* Thorne is right. I should get to the point."
Consuelo set down her cup, opened the saddlebag the cup
had been in, and slid her hand inside. "It saddens me but
we do what we must, eh?"

"What saddens you, you boring bitch?" Thorne asked.

"This." Consuelo pulled a Merwin & Bray pocket pistol
from the saddlebag and shot Thorne between the eyes.

22

Charlie and Esteban gaped in astonishment. It was Charlie who woke up first and grabbed for his Smith & Wesson. He had it half out when Consuelo shot him in the eye.

"No, *senorita*!" Esteban cried. He was fast. His ivory-handled Remington was almost level when the Merwin & Bray boomed and his forehead burst in a fine spray.

In the quiet that followed, Consuelo said, "Him, I did not want to do. He was nice to me."

"Hell," Fargo said.

"One day, perhaps," Consuelo said. "I very much doubt they let whores into heaven."

"You came back for the money," Fargo guessed.

"But of course." Consuelo stood and trained her pocket pistol on him. "I am sorry, handsome one. But there can not be witnesses." She thumbed back the hammer.

Fargo had faced death before. He'd faced it so many times that he didn't flinch when he found himself staring into the muzzle of her pistol. All he did was say, "So much for the good times we had in San Gabriel."

Consuelo smiled. "We did, didn't we? You are a magnificent lover."

"We should do it again sometime."

Her smile became a sad one. "I would like to let you live. Truly I would. But if I do, you will report me to the Texas Rangers."

"For shooting three killers I was going to shoot anyway?"

"For taking the money they were paid," Consuelo said.

"It's not my money."

"It is nine thousand dollars," Consuelo said. "A thousand for each of them was the agreed amount." She lowered her pistol. "It's not a fortune but it is more than I could save in a lifetime. It is enough for me to start a new life in San Francisco."

"Go start it," Fargo said.

Consuelo studied him as if seeking to see into his soul. "Do I dare? Can I trust you?"

"All I want," Fargo said, "is to know who paid them." As if he couldn't guess.

Consuelo shook her head.

"Why not?"

"I gave my word. Not that I am part of it. I am only a whore."

"And a cook is only a cook."

"Senor?"

"You can break your word," Fargo said.

"Would you break yours?"

Fargo frowned. She had him there. Whenever he gave his word, he invariably did his best to keep it.

"I didn't think so," Consuelo said. "So you cannot blame me if I keep mine." She went around the fire, picked up the money pouch, and slung the strap over her shoulder. Patting it, she laughed. "Why I didn't take it in the first place, I will never know."

"Cut me loose," Fargo said, "and we'll go our separate ways."

Consuelo bent and reached for a knife on Thorne's hip then straightened without sliding it from its sheath. "No," she said.

"I'd be obliged."

"No," Consuelo said again. "Letting you live is dangerous enough. To free you would be too trusting."

"What if I give you my word?"

Consuelo grinned. "Nice try, as you gringos say. But I
think it is wise to buy myself time. It will take you a while
to free yourself and by then I will be long gone."

Fargo didn't mention that he could track her down as
easily as he'd tracked the outlaws. Or that it wouldn't take
long at all to get free.

As if she could read his thoughts, Consuelo took
Thorne's knife and threw it as far as she could. "Good luck
finding it."

Fargo didn't care. There were other ways.

Consuelo slid the pocket pistol into her saddlebag. She
picked up the coffeepot in both hands and held it over the fire.
"Was this how you were going to free yourself? By holding
the rope to the flames?" So saying, she upended the pot.

There was a loud hiss and a tremendous amount of
smoke, and when it cleared, the fire was out.

Consuelo let the pot drop. It hit with a clang and rolled.

"Oh, well," Fargo said.

Stooping, Consuelo cupped his chin and looked him in
the eyes. *"Lo siento."*

"Sure you are."

"I am truly sorry," Consuelo insisted. "You will find a
way. You are big and strong."

"If some Comanches or Apaches come along, I'll be
easy pickings."

"The chances are slim. But if they do, it is God's will,
and there is nothing I can do."

"Handy having God to blame," Fargo said. "Will it help
you sleep better?"

"Be nice," Consuelo scolded. "You are still breathing, are
you not?" She walked to her horse, hooked the pouch strap
over her saddle horn, and came back for her saddlebags. As
she bent, she smiled and said, "I will take the horses, too.
Where is yours? It must be nearby."

"You don't want to do that," Fargo said.

"Yes, I do. I will find your animal and take it with me. It's a long walk to the ranch but you might make it." Consuelo straightened. "Should it be that you can't get free and you die of thirst, do not think poorly of me."

"And don't you think poorly of me," Fargo said.

"Why would I?"

Whipping his legs up and around, Fargo slammed them against the back of hers. Squawking, she upended and landed hard on her back. She made a sound like an alley cat about to attack, and shook her head to clear it.

Fargo drew his legs up and rammed his heels into her jaw. She fell back but she wasn't out. Rolling over, she weakly tried to crawl off.

"You brought this on yourself," Fargo said, and brought his boots crashing down on the top of her head. He tried not to do it too hard.

Consuelo whimpered and stopped moving.

Fargo set to work on the rope. With the fire extinguished and Thorne's knife gone, that left one way. Sitting up, he pried at the rope around his ankles. Not at the knots, which would take forever to loosen. He tried to slide the rope high enough up that he could reach into his boot and palm the Arkansas toothpick.

The rope was tight as hell. He tugged. He tried to wriggle it. He pressed his fingertips to it. At first it barely moved. Then it moved by fractions. He was at it a good ten minutes when he felt it give way, if only slightly.

Working it up and down, Fargo felt it move a little more.

Consuelo groaned.

Fargo's fingers hurt like hell and one was bleeding from under the nail. He gripped and pulled, the angle awkward because his hands were behind his back. His shoulder protested. His wrists ached.

Suddenly the rope slid above his boots. Wasting no time, he hiked his pant leg. Two strokes of the toothpick was all it took. His legs were free. His wrists quickly followed.

His Colt lay near Thorne's body. Retrieving it, he brushed dust off the barrel and checked that there were five pills in the wheel. As he twirled it into his holster, Consuelo opened her eyes.

"You hurt me."

"You're alive."

Gingerly placing a hand on her chin, Consuelo winced. "You almost broke my jaw. And my head. So much pain."

"I tried to go easy on you."

"*Bastardo*. I let you live and you attacked me."

"No one steals my horse."

"*That* is why?"

"If you'd taken it, I'd have hunted you down."

"So, what are you saying? That you have done me a favor by stopping me?"

"Do you like breathing?"

Consuelo started, and blinked. "I see. Your horse means that much to you?" She went to sit up and reached for her saddlebags.

"Ah-ah," Fargo said. He grabbed them before she could make a try for her pocket pistol.

"You are not the man I thought you were if you would kill me over a horse," Consuelo said.

Fargo gathered up the six-shooters belonging to Thorne and company and threw them as she had thrown the knife.

"Stay put while I fetch my horse."

He knew she wouldn't. He knew exactly what she would do. He had her saddlebags and the knife, but the money pouch was on her saddle horn. So he wasn't at all surprised that he'd gone barely twenty feet when she hollered and yipped and he turned to see her lashing her animal to the west.

"I wish you luck," Fargo said. She'd need it. A woman alone, in hostile country, with outlaws as common as fleas, and her with all that money.

141

In five minutes he was in the saddle himself. He didn' bother with the bodies but he did take their horses. There was no need for the animals to suffer.

It was a long ride, giving him time to ponder. Abou being used, being shot at, being nearly killed. Someone had a lot to answer for, and he thought he knew who.

The temperature climbed. By noon he was sweltering. He perked up when he came across a few cows. It meant he was close. He saw more, but no cowhands. Not a cowboy any where. That puzzled him.

When, at last, splashes of pink broke the monotony, he tapped his spurs and arrived at a gallop. No one was to be seen, which added to his puzzlement.

Going to the ranch house, he wearily dismounted. He didn't knock. He hurried down the hall and nearly collided with Miquel, who came scampering out of the parlor.

"*Senor!* I thought I heard a noise."

"Where is everyone?" Fargo asked, and specifically mentioned, "Miss Caventry and her brother?" Not that he gave a damn about Lester.

"They are gone, *senor.*"

"They're on their way home?"

"No, *senor,*" Miquel said. "They went with *Senora* Patterson and the *vaqueros.*"

"Went where?"

"After the *bandidos* who attacked us and killed poor Lupe and *Senor* Bronack and the rest."

"All the bandits are dead," Fargo said, "and I didn't see any sign of your mistress or her punchers on my way here. Are you sure that's where they went?"

"*Si, senor. Senora* Patterson got word that the *bandidos* were hiding along the river to the south and she took all the cowboys with her. The *captaz,* the foreman, tried to talk her out of going but she wouldn't listen. She can be most fierce when she is mad."

"Miss Caventry and her brother asked to go with them?"

"Oh, no, *senor*. They wanted to stay. The brother, in particular, argued most bitterly. But *Senora* Patterson insisted. She said it would not be safe for them to stay here alone."

"Son of a bitch," Fargo said.

"Senor?"

"There are some horses out front. See that they're taken care of."

Fargo hurried out, climbed on the Ovaro, and once more resorted to his spurs.

As with the raiders, the tracks were easy to follow.

Fargo rode hard. Dandy was in danger and didn't know it. And if anything happened to her, there would be hell to pay.

23

Their camp was in a bend of the Rio Grande, in thick growth that hid them from unfriendly eyes. But then they went and made a fire big enough that the smoke could be seen for miles.

Fargo was glad they were careless. He didn't need to track them the last few miles. He just rode to the smoke.

Two punchers had been posted as sentries, one on the riverbank, the other where the belt of vegetation met the prairie.

Fargo drew rein before he was spotted. The oak case was too long to fit all the way in his saddlebag, and he wanted to hide it. Loosening his bedroll, he slid the case in, then retied the roll so it wouldn't slide out. Other than a slight bulge, it wasn't noticeable. Satisfied, he rode on in.

The cowboy standing guard jerked a rifle up, and promptly lowered it again. "I know who you are," he said.

"Any luck finding the men who attacked the ranch?" Fargo asked.

"Brazos and most of the hands are out searchin'," the puncher revealed. "Mrs. Patterson says it's only a matter of time."

"Isn't everything?" Fargo said.

The great lady herself was seated on a folding chair by the fire. She wore a riding habit and high boots and was drinking from a long-stemmed glass.

Dandy and Lester were with her. Sister and brother

ppeared equally glum. Dandy perked up, though, when he saw Fargo, and hurried over to meet him. "You're safe, thank God."

Fargo dismounted. For a moment he thought she was going to throw her arms around him and kiss him. "You missed me?"

"I worried about you, yes," she confessed.

Sarah Patterson didn't bother to stand. She did raise her glass and show her dazzling smile. "Look who it is. How did your hunt go?"

"I'd rather hear about yours," Fargo said.

"No luck, huh?" Sarah said. "That's because you were wasting your time. Word reached me that they were seen in this area, and I brought every hand I could gather to help me root them out."

Fargo wondered how much "rooting" she was doing while sitting on her ass around a fire, but he didn't bring it up. "What is that you're drinking?"

"Wine," Sarah said, and took a sip. "I offered some to my guests but they're both in a funk."

"Can you blame me?" Dandy said. "If I don't recover the bowie, my father is out fifty thousand dollars."

"So are we," Lester said glumly.

"We'll get the knife back," Sarah told them. "Wait and see."

Fargo admired how glibly she lied. "You're not off searching with your men?"

"I'm the general, not one of the troops," Sarah said. "My foreman will let me know when they come across anything important."

Fargo looked around. "I thought Consuelo might be with you. I didn't see her at the ranch."

Without batting an eye, Sarah said, "She went back to San Gabriel. She never stays long at the Bar P."

"Ah," Fargo said, as if he believed her.

"It's good to get away for a while," Sarah remarked,

gazing about at the trees and the river. "I like the exercise
She drained her glass in a gulp and let out a contented sig]

"Do you ever miss having a husband?" Fargo asked.

Sarah's head snapped toward him so fast, it was a wor
der her neck didn't break. "Where the hell did that com
from?"

"Didn't you tell me you've had four so far? A woma
who's had that many must like being married." Fargo onl
meant to get her talking about her last one, Charlie. But h
struck a richer vein.

"You've got it backwards," Sarah said. "It was four to
many. I can do without men, but they have their uses." Sh
beckoned, and a puncher took a wine bottle from a wicke
basket and refilled her glass. Only after she'd downed
third of it at another swallow did she say, "Not all of us a
born into money."

"What does that mean?" Dandy asked.

"I should think it would be obvious," Sarah replie
"Some of us have to work our way up from nothing. Take m
for instance. Each of my spouses was richer than the last."

"Am I to understand that you deserted them for greene
pastures?" Dandy asked.

"No," Sarah replied. "They died."

"All four?"

Sarah shrugged. "Men don't live as long as wome
Everyone knows that."

"But all four?" Dandy had focused on what was goin
through Fargo's mind, as well.

"It happens," Sarah said. "My first one got drunk and fe
down a flight of stairs and broke his fool neck. My secon
was kicked by a horse. My third died in his sleep. His hear
the doctor said. And finally there was poor Charlie."

"Not so poor," Fargo said.

Sarah grinned. "True. He became sickly and weak an
just faded away. The doctor never could figure out why."

Fargo noticed a coffeepot on a flat rock. He got his ti

146

up, and as he was filling it, he casually asked, "How long fter Charlie died did Consuelo start paying you visits?"

Sarah froze in the act of taking another swallow. "You sk the strangest damn things."

"I don't suppose you're going to tell me?"

"I don't suppose I am."

"All this gab," Lester said, "bores the hell out of me."

"Poor baby," Sarah said. "Why can't you be more like our sister instead of a pain in the ass?"

"Go to hell, bitch."

"Lester!" Dandy exclaimed. "We're her guests."

"That's all right, sweetie," Sarah said. "He's male. He an't help himself. They're next to hopeless, except for one hing."

"What thing?" Dandy asked.

"You're next to hopeless, too," Sarah said sweetly.

Behind his cup, Fargo frowned. He was annoyed at imself. He should have caught on sooner. It explained the our husbands, and a lot more.

"Why am I hopeless?" Dandy was asking.

"You don't see men for what they are." Sarah gulped nore wine.

Fargo wondered if it was the fruit of the vine that was oosening her tongue.

"I'm not exactly sure what you mean," Dandy said. Some men are nice, some aren't. So what? Women are the ame way."

"No, dear. All men are pigs. Plain and simple. They want ne thing from women, and use us to their own ends."

"That's preposterous," Dandy said. "My father is as kind person as ever drew breath."

"You forget I've met—" Sarah said, and caught herself.

"Oh. That's right. Didn't you say you ran into him in ustin?"

"Yes," Sarah answered, reluctantly, it seemed to Fargo. I had business to attend to in the capital. One night I attended the theater and there he was. We exchanged a few pleasantries."

Lester, who had his chin in his hand and couldn't be bothered to take part in their talk, raised his head. "Wait a minute. He told me about that trip. You weren't the woman who was badgering him, were you?"

"Badgering?" Dandy repeated.

Lester nodded. "He said that some woman pestered him no end about going out. She practically threw herself at him, was how he put it."

"That wasn't me," Sarah said.

"Father wasn't interested," Lester told his sister. "He confided in me that he thought the woman was a shrew."

A slight flush tinged Sarah's face.

"It just hit me," Fargo chimed in, "that your father is one of the few men in Texas richer than Charlie Patterson used to be."

"What does that have to do with anything?" Sarah angrily asked.

"Beats me," Fargo said.

Dandy smoothed her dress and plucked at a piece of lint. "Whoever that woman was, she wasted her time. Father hasn't so much as looked at another woman since Mother died. They were very much in love." She smiled at Sarah. "That's how I know you're wrong about men. I've seen how Father was with her. Very caring. Very considerate."

"Listen, dearie—" Sarah began, but got no further.

The rumble of hooves heralded the return of Brazos and the punchers. They forded the river fifty yards east of the camp and brought their dusty, dripping mounts to a stop in the clearing.

Brazos was first off and strode over. "I hate to have to disappoint you, ma'am."

"You still can't find them?" Sarah said.

"Not hide nor hair." The foreman nodded at Fargo. "We did find tracks of unshod horses. A Comanche hunting

148

party, we reckon." He paused. "Oh. And I sent Clay south to fetch those other fellers like you wanted."

"Good." Sarah turned to Fargo. "Looks like it'll be up to you to find the men who attacked my ranch."

"I don't work for you," Fargo said.

"But you're a scout, a tracker. And they stole what belongs to the woman you do work for."

"Her pa hired me."

Dandy was as surprised as Sarah. "I should think you would want to help him by finding the knife."

"He hired me to guide you across the badlands," Fargo said. "Nothing more."

"But you went after the outlaws on your own," Dandy reminded him. "Why not help out now?"

Fargo decided to twist the knife, so to speak, and see what happened. "No need." Rising, he stepped to the Ovaro, untied his bedroll, and brought it back.

"You're taking a nap?" Sarah scoffed.

Kneeling, Fargo unrolled it. At the sight of the oak case, Dandy squealed in delight and Lester jumped up as if pricked by a pin.

Sarah Patterson was a portrait in barely suppressed fury. "How in hell did you get hold of that?"

"I found the men who took it."

Dandy was ecstatic. Opening the case, she ran her hand along the bowie and beamed. "This is wonderful. I can't thank you enough. Father will be so pleased."

"The only one who won't," Fargo mentioned, staring at Sarah, "is the person who put them up to taking it."

If looks could kill, he'd be dead where he stood.

24

Dandy was so excited at having the knife back, she wanted to head to the ranch for her things and leave before nightfall for home.

"Don't be silly," Sarah sought to dissuade her. "Once again it's too late in the day. Use your head and wait until morning."

"I don't want any more delays."

"For once I agree with my sister," Lester said. "Let's get the hell out of here."

"If you insist," Sarah said unhappily. "I'll have some of my men escort you to the ranch."

"That won't be necessary. We have Skye to look after us." Dandy turned to him. "We do, don't we?"

"I was paid to get you here and back," Fargo said.

"You don't mind if we leave right this minute?"

"Just so you savvy that you're to do as I say at all times."

Dandy closed the case and patted it. "Do you expect more trouble? Didn't you say all of them are dead?"

"How many times have we been attacked?" Fargo reminded her. "Whoever is behind it might take it into their head to try again."

"All the more reason for us to go," Lester said. "I hate all this gallivanting around. I want to be in my own room, sleep in my own bed, eat food I like to eat."

"What's wrong with the food I've had our cook serve?" Sarah demanded.

"Nothing. She's just not *our* cook."

Sarah had her punchers saddle the mounts the Caventrys were using. Up to the moment they climbed on, she tried her best to talk them out of leaving. She even offered to ride to the ranch with them if they'd only stay the night.

"I'm sorry, but no," Dandy said. "It's high time we left."

Fargo had waited until that moment to mention what everyone else had overlooked. "Besides, you can't leave. You're overseeing the hunt for the killers."

Brazos reacted as if he'd been socked on the jaw. "Say, that's right. You must know where they are if you stole the case from them."

"They're dead," Fargo said.

"You found them and killed them? Were they somewhere nearby?" Brazos asked.

"They were as far north of the ranch as you are south of it."

"How can that be?"

Fargo smiled at Sarah Patterson. "Ask your boss. Maybe she can explain." He tapped his spurs, and Dandy and Lester followed. Twisting, he looked back.

Sarah Patterson appeared fit to explode but she smiled and waved. Her eyes were twin spikes in Fargo's back.

"God Almighty, I'm glad to be shed of that woman," Lester said. "She's too damned bossy."

"Don't be so hard on her," Dandy chided. "She only has our best interests at heart."

Fargo couldn't help thinking that if Dandy was as good at telling the age of knives as she was at reading people, there was no way in hell the bowie was genuine.

Twilight was mantling the prairie when they drew rein at the hitch rail at the ranch house.

Ever-dutiful Miquel waited on the Caventrys hand and foot. He offered to have Esmeralda prepare a quick meal, and over Lester's objections, Dandy accepted.

"I don't want to ride half the night on an empty stomach," she explained.

Neither did Fargo. The pair didn't know it yet but this would be the last they got to relax for a considerable spell. While they waited in the parlor for the food to cook, he went out on the porch and scanned the horizon to the south. So far there was no sign of pursuit.

He went to the stable. Their packhorse was in a stall at the rear. He brought it out, tied on their packs, and brought the horse to the house.

The meal took longer than he liked.

Lester, who had complained about having to eat, was the one who dawdled.

Finally Fargo stood up and announced that he and Dandy were leaving, and Lester could come or not.

Night had fallen. A host of stars shimmered in the Texas sky. Now and then a coyote raised a lament, and over by the woodshed an owl hooted.

"How safe is it to ride in the dark?" Lester asked as they passed the last of the outbuildings. "I haven't done much of it."

"It's safer than staying here," Fargo said.

"Why are you so convinced we'll have more trouble?" Dandy asked.

"Because I have a hunch this was never about the knife."

"Then what?"

"We'll talk later." Fargo wanted to put as much distance as he could behind them. He brought the Ovaro to a trot and heard Dandy say something he didn't catch.

The country was mostly open. They encountered a lot of cows, usually bunched up and bedded down.

Lester was his usual wonderful self. He complained that he couldn't see well in the dark. He complained that the breeze made him cold. He complained when Fargo informed them that they weren't going to stop until about midnight.

Fargo abided it as long as he could and ended the bitching with a flat, "Shut the hell up, boy."

It was ten o'clock, or thereabouts, when Dandy brought her horse up and raised her voice to say, "We're not heading for San Gabriel, are we?"

"Figured that out, did you?"

"I know the Big Dipper points at the North Star and we've been riding toward it since we started." Dandy paused. "San Gabriel is to the west."

"They'll expect us to go that way and lose half a day or more before they realize their mistake."

"Who will?" Dandy studied him. "Why do I have the feeling you're playing some sort of game?" She didn't wait for an answer. "Be honest with me. What are our chances of making it home alive?"

"It depends on how many come after us."

An hour and a half later Fargo decided they had come far enough. He'd prefer a cold camp but Dandy mentioned how hungry she was and Lester grumbled that he couldn't get to sleep "without something warm in my belly."

Fargo kindled a small fire in a gully. He put beans on, and despite the late hour, coffee to wash it down. As they sat waiting, Dandy cleared her throat.

"Don't you think it's time you told us what's going on?"

"You know things we don't, don't you?" Lester said.

"I have hunches," Fargo said. "If she sends more gun hands after us, then it proves I'm right."

"She?" Lester said.

"Don't be stupid," Dandy said. "Who else but Sarah Patterson? Why would she want us dead, though? That makes no sense."

"She knows I suspect," Fargo said.

"Suspect *what*, for God's sake?" Lester asked.

"That she doesn't take no for an answer."

"Oh, that explained a lot," Lester said glibly, and swore. Dandy turned. "Will you shut up and let him finish?"

"It's like this," Fargo began. "She's had four husbands. Each was richer than the last. And it could be their deaths weren't accidents or natural."

"You're saying she killed them?"

"And the man who ran the Mexican rancho she made part of the Bar P, and some of his *vaqueros*. Who knows how many others?"

"But why would she want us dead? I'm sure as hell not going to marry her," Lester said.

"Neither is your pa, and that's why you're sitting there."

"Oh, my God." Dandy grasped what he was saying. "Her trip to Austin!"

Fargo nodded. "She set her sights on your father and went there to woo him. Only he wasn't interested. For once her charms didn't work."

"But he wasn't mean to her or anything," Lester said. "He told me himself that he was firm but gentle when he refused her invites to her room. His very words."

"Her room?" Dandy said.

"Gentle or not," Fargo remarked, "Sarah Patterson took it as an insult. Some ladies do. They get so mad, they're out for blood."

Dandy's forehead was furrowed in thought. "When she contacted him about the knife, was she hoping she could change his mind?"

"The only thing she wants with him now," Fargo said, "is to make him suffer."

"How?" Lester asked skeptically. "By selling him a knife that didn't really belong to Jim Bowie?"

"Don't you get it yet?" Dandy answered before Fargo could. "All the attempts on our lives. She intends to make Father pay for spurning her by doing us in."

"That's far-fetched, don't you think?" Lester responded. "Who goes to that extreme?"

"She does," Fargo said.

Lester considered that, and said, "Hold on a minute.

Those first bandits were after the money they thought we were carrying."

"She didn't know you had a bank draft."

"Once she found out we did," Dandy said, "the next bunch she sent tried to kill us outright."

"But they took the damn knife," Lester said.

"To make it seem that was what they were after," Fargo explained. "In case your father sent the law to look into it."

"Dear God, she's devious," Dandy said.

Lester was still dubious. "All this is guesswork. You don't have any proof."

"We'll know tomorrow or the next day whether I'm right or not," Fargo said.

"How?"

"Another pack of curly wolves will be out to blast us to pieces."

25

They came riding hard and purposeful out of the south. That there were eight of them wasn't a surprise. That one was a woman shouldn't have surprised Fargo but did.

"There are so many," Dandy said, unable to keep the fear out of her voice.

Lester gulped. "You and your goddamn hunches," he growled at Fargo.

They were on their bellies at the rim of a low bluff, the only eminence for miles around.

"We have an edge," Fargo said.

"Because we're higher than they are?" Lester sscoffed.

"No," Fargo said. "Our edge is that they don't know we know."

Lester, as usual, didn't savvy. "What difference does that make? They'll shoot us to ribbons. Or whatever horrible end that bitch has in store for us."

"Why is she with them?" Dandy wondered. "Why take the risk?"

"You keep forgetting," Fargo said. "She's killed about half a dozen men, maybe more. She likes it. She likes to see their faces as they die."

"You don't know that," Lester said.

"It would make her a monster," Dandy declared. "A living, breathing monster."

"Not for long," Fargo said. Not if he could help it. He started to slide back but Dandy put her hand on his arm.

"Hold on. You're fixing to kill her?"

"She's fixing to kill us."

"But she's female," Dandy said. "Shouldn't we try to take her alive and turn her over to the law?"

"You can if you want," Fargo said. "Me, I'm blowing her brains out."

Lester laughed. "At last we agree on something."

The south side of the bluff was a sheer face of dirt and rocks but the north end had long since buckled, creating a slope overgrown with grass. Fargo went down it in long bounds to their horses at the bottom. The siblings came slower.

Shucking the Henry, Fargo fed a cartridge in. "You two stay here."

"Can't we help?" Dandy asked, and patted her handbag. "I have my six-shooter."

"Only if they get past me." Fargo ran back to the top and flattened a yard from the rim so Patterson and her killers wouldn't see him.

They weren't quite in range yet.

Fargo wished he had his old Sharps. With it he could pick them off at three times the distance. But he'd stopped using it because it was a single-shot, and in a tight spot, sixteen rounds beat one round any day.

He fixed a bead on the lead rider, a man in a sombrero who kept leaning to one side or the other. A tracker, he reckoned.

There wasn't much of a breeze so he didn't have to take the wind into account. And since he was only thirty feet up, the elevation wasn't much of a factor, either.

The tracker drew rein. When the rest came up, he pointed at the bluff and said something to Sarah Patterson.

To Fargo's consternation, they spread out. In a bunch they'd be easier to drop. A skirmish line could get in close before he could drop them.

Fargo was tempted to scramble back down and fan the

breeze. But no. This was the spot he'd picked for his stand, and here it would be.

He didn't recognize any of the riders. None were Bar P cowhands. They must be the men Sarah had sent Clay south to fetch. More gun hands, most likely.

Fargo had no compunctions about putting lead into them. They were out for his blood, and to make worm food of the Caventrys. They had it coming.

Sarah and the tracker were close together, the rest spaced out about ten yards apart. She waved an arm and started forward at a trot.

The tracker was Fargo's first target. He held his breath to steady his body and was curling his finger around the trigger when fate played a dirty trick. The sun must have reflected off the Henry's barrel or the brass receiver because the tracker stiffened and hollered and suddenly swung onto the side of his roan, Comanche-fashion.

The other riders raked their spurs. Revolvers were swept from holsters, rifles were pointed at the bluff.

"Damn," Fargo said, and shot a man in a brown hat .

All hell erupted.

The riders unleashed a firestorm. Slugs smacked the bluff, high and low.

Some of the riders bent to make themselves harder to hit. Others charged recklessly, shooting as fast as they could shoot.

Fargo fired and a man reeled. He fired a second time and another tumbled over his mount's rump.

By now they knew exactly where he was. All their lead came uncomfortably close. They were trying to keep him pinned down so they could reach the bluff.

Instead, Fargo rose up, fired, and flattened. Rose up, fired, and flattened. He dropped only two of the seven, and there was Sarah, yet.

Lead thumped and thudded and clipped the grass. When the spray slackened, he rose up for another shot.

Nearly all the riders were to the bluff. One pointed a Spencer.

Fargo cored his head.

"Up there!!" Sarah bellowed. "A thousand extra dollars to whoever kills the son of a bitch."

A gun boomed. Not at the south end of the bluff, where the killers were, but at the north end, where Fargo had left Dandy and her brother.

Heaving to his feet, Fargo raced down the slope. Halfway, he saw Dandy in a crouch, holding her revolver two-handed as she fired.

Lester was in the middle of the horses, gripping a saddle horn as if about to mount or because he was so scared he couldn't stand on his own two legs. The whites of his eyes were showing.

Fargo ran to Dandy and she glanced up and smiled.

"Just in time," she yelled. "I'm holding them back but I'm about empty."

A slug caught her in the shoulder and drilled out her back in a shower of blood and flesh and dress. It spun her around, and she dropped her six-shooter and cried out in agony.

The killer who had shot her was about to fire again.

Fargo sent lead through the man's brain. Bending, he wrapped his left arm around Dandy and pulled her toward the horses.

"My pistol!"

"Forget the damn gun." Fargo shoved her toward the horses and spun, just in time.

Two assassins were converging. One fired and Fargo's hat went flying.

Quick as thought Fargo dropped him. He dropped the second. As he pumped the lever, Dandy screamed his name.

Another shooter was coming around the other side of the bluff. They both squeezed trigger at the instant they set eyes on each other. Fargo felt a sting in his leg. The shooter jolted to a halt with a new hole about where his heart should be.

Dandy screamed a second time.

Fargo tried to turn but he was too slow. A blow to the head pitched him to his knees. Another smashed the Henry from his hands. He clawed for the Colt but it was snatched from his holster.

"We have him, *senora*. Alive, as you wanted."

It was the tracker. He had dark eyes and a neatly trimmed beard, and his gun belt was decorated with silver conchos.

Sarah Patterson came from behind him. She, too, wore a gun belt, but she hadn't drawn her six-gun. She smirked at Fargo, and at Dandy on her knees a few yards away. "Well, well, well," she said.

Fargo was struggling to collect his wits. He still had the Arkansas toothpick in its ankle sheath. The trick was to palm it without being seen.

"You put up a good fight, I'll say that for you," Sarah said.

"Go to hell," Fargo got out.

Sarah made a clucking sound. "Now, now. I'm being civil. You can be too." She turned toward the horses, and Lester. "And there's your worthless excuse for a brother, my dear. Cowering, I see."

Dandy, her hand over her wound, blood oozing between her fingers, groaned and said, "How could you?"

"How could I what?" Sarah placed her hands on her hips. "How could I go to so much trouble and expense to put your father in his place?"

"So Skye was right," Dandy gasped. "This is about revenge."

"Never anything else," Sarah said. "I'm used to having my own way. To always getting what I want. I picked your father for husband number five but he refused to have anything to do with me." She swore. "No one treats me like that. Especially a man."

"You lured us here with the bowie to kill us?" Dandy said. "Is that how you want our father to suffer?"

"To tell the truth, dearie, I figured your pa would come himself. I had plans for him. It involved a fire and a branding iron. I can't tell you how disappointed I was when he wrote me that he was sending you and your harebrained brother."

"You're hideous," Dandy said.

Sarah found that hilarious. After she was done laughing she said, "What I am is a woman scorned."

Fargo had eased his fingers to his right boot. All he needed was a moment's distraction.

"You won't get away with this," Dandy said through clenched teeth. "My father has influence. He'll contact the Rangers."

"Who will report back that you were murdered by bandits. I'll have half a dozen people willing to testify to that effect."

"What now?" Dandy asked. "You finish us off?"

The tall Mexican was listening to their exchange, and pointed his six-gun at her.

"You sure are anxious to die," Sarah said. "Any last words before Emilio, here, puts one between your eyes?"

Fargo saw Lester come up unnoticed behind her and was momentarily rooted in shock at what he saw Lester was holding.

"I have a couple of last words," Lester said.

Sarah snorted and began to turn. "What do you have to say, boy?"

"Die, bitch," Lester screamed, and drove the bowie into her vitals.

Sarah Patterson shrieked.

Emilio leveled his revolver at Lester but before he could shoot, Fargo jumped erect and thrust the toothpick into his chest below the sternum. Once, twice, a third stab, and Emilio melted.

For a long minute afterward none of them spoke. They watched the bodies convulse and the blood pools mingle.

"Guess I taught her," Lester said, puffing out his chest.

"Can you stop preening and help me?" Dandy said. "I need bandaging before I bleed to death." She wearily smiled up at Fargo. "How about you, Skye?"

"I need a drink," Fargo said.

LOOKING FORWARD!
The following is the opening section of the next novel in the exciting *Trailsman* series from Signet:

TRAILSMAN #382
TERROR TRACKDOWN

1861, just over the Divide—someone makes the mistake of stealing a certain Ovaro.

The wolves came out of the timber at a run.

Skye Fargo wasn't expecting trouble. He had crossed the Divide over Berthoud Pass and was winding down Clear Creek Canyon toward the Fraser River. Lower down were the foothills and the distant city of Denver.

The only things on his mind were whiskey, cards, and women, not necessarily in that order. A big man, wide at the shoulders and slim at the hips, he wore buckskins, boots, and a high-crowned hat, along with a red bandanna and a Colt that had seen a lot of use. He was looking forward to a week without a care in the world. He planned to spend it indulging in what some would call wild shenanigans and others would brand outright sinful. He aimed to get lucky, get drunk, and get laid, and again, not necessarily in that order.

The army's campaign against a band of Modocs had taken a lot out of him. The renegades proved hard to find and once found, proved that they were serious about fighting the white man to the last warrior. Now Fargo had time to himself, and he couldn't wait to taste the treats that gave his life spice.

When three wolves broke out of pines about two hundred yards to the south, Fargo wasn't alarmed. Wolves hardly ever went after people. They didn't attack horses often, either.

At first sight he figured they were after deer or some other game. But then he saw that they weren't paralleling the tree line. They were coming straight toward him. They were coming fast, too.

Bodies low to the ground, ears back, their tails straight, they flew toward him and the Ovaro in a beeline that left no doubt as to their purpose.

"What the hell?" Fargo blurted. He thought about jerking his Henry rifle from the saddle scabbard, but why bother? The Ovaro had a big enough lead that it could outrun them. Jabbing his spurs, he brought the stallion to a gallop.

They were on a flat stretch but soon he came to a slope and had to slow. Glancing back, he saw that the wolves were about a hundred and fifty yards away, give or take a few. He flew down the slope to another flat and used his spurs.

It wasn't half a minute later that he glanced back again and realized he had miscalculated. The wolves weren't directly behind him, they were closing at an angle. Already they'd cut the distance to a hundred and twenty yards and now they were coming on even faster.

"Damn." Fargo urged the Ovaro to its peak and realized something else.

The stallion was tired. They'd been on the go for a lot of

days, from sunrise to sunset, pushing hard over some of the most rugged country on the continent.

Still, Fargo had unbounded confidence in his mount. The Ovaro had saved his hash more times than he could count. Its stamina was exceptional. Even tired, it should be able to leave the wolves breathing its dust.

But when Fargo looked over his shoulder yet again, the wolves were another twenty to thirty yards nearer. They were big and in their prime and over short distances they could bring down a moose or an elk.

Or a horse.

His jaw muscles twitching in anger, Fargo rode as if the Ovaro's life depended on it. Which it did.

They'd been through too much together. Some folks might deem it silly but he regarded the stallion as more of a pard than an animal. It was a friend, and he'd be damned if he'd let anything happen to it.

Another slope loomed. This one was steeper and littered with boulders, forcing Fargo to slow even more. At the bottom he snapped his head around and genuine worry blossomed.

The wolves weren't more than eighty yards away.

"Son of a bitch."

Fargo began to think about making a stand. Find a spot he could defend and resort to the Henry. If he picked the fastest wolf off, the rest might scatter. He'd tangled with wolves before. Most were spooked by the sound of gunfire.

That gave him an idea. Drawing his Colt, he shifted in the saddle. He doubted he'd hit them but he fired two swift shots anyway, hoping the blasts would bring them to a stop or cause them to veer away.

No such luck. The three lupine killers came on as determinedly as ever.

Fargo swore more colorfully. He'd gone from being

angry to outright mad. He shoved the Colt into his holster and concentrated on riding.

The next time he glanced back the wolves were only sixty yards back.

Fargo needed to find a spot soon. He was at a narrow point in the valley, with forest to the north and the south. Trying to reach it would be pointless. Heavy timber would slow the Ovaro even more, and give the wolves the advantage of cover. He needed to fight them in the open.

Ahead was an ideal spot. maybe half an acre in extent There were a few boulders but they were small and a few trees but they were far apart.

"There," he said to himself.

On reaching it, Fargo hauled on the reins so sharply, the Ovaro slid to a stop on its haunches. He was out of the saddle before the stallion stopped moving, yanking on the Henry as he swung down. He worked the lever to feed a cartridge into the chamber, dropped to a knee, and took deliberate aim at the foremost wolf.

By now the wolves were only forty yards away.

Fargo heard the Ovaro whinny and assumed it was because of the three wolves he was about to shoot. Then the stallion whinnied again and he risked a quick glance to find out why and his blood became ice in his veins.

Two more wolves were closing from the north.

It was a typical tactic. A pack split and converged on prey from two or more directions. And while the prey was focused on one group, the rest rushed in close enough for the kill.

Fargo should have kept a lookout for more. He fixed a quick bead on the first wolf to the west and smoothly stroked the trigger. At the boom, the wolf went into a roll but was on its paws again in a twinkling and running strong

Fargo worked the lever to fire again. Things had gone to

ell and now it was do or die. He fired and the first wolf's
egs buckled and it slid to a stop and this time it didn't rise.

Whirling, Fargo snapped a shot at the wolves to the
north but he must have missed because the wolf he shot at
didn't slow or stumble.

This was bad. Four wolves, two thirty yards to the west
and two about the same to the north. Grim ravagers, out to
bring the Ovaro down no matter what. Odds were he
couldn't drop all four before the wolves were on them.

Fargo took a step back thinking that if he vaulted onto
the stallion and rode like hell he still might be able to get
away but then his left heel struck a rock he hadn't noticed,
and before he could catch himself, he fell. He landed on his
back and instantly twisted to rise.

The wolves were so close he could see the gleam of
bloodlust in their eyes.

Snapping the Henry to his shoulder, Fargo fired. The
wolf he shot at yelped and broke stride but didn't go down.
He worked the lever and fired again and now there were
only three but three was more than enough, and the wolves
had reached them.

Another whinny shattered the air as Fargo jacked the
lever. He hadn't quite worked it all the way when a hairy
form slammed into him with the impact of an avalanche.
The next moment he was flat on the ground with a wolf
straddling him, and the only thing keeping the wolf's sla-
vering jaws from his throat was the Henry, which he had
shoved against the wolf's throat.

The Ovaro whinnied louder than ever.

Fargo could only imagine what was happening. The
wolves would go for the stallion's legs, and if they broke
one, or got a good hold, they'd bring it down and go for its
neck or its belly.

Fear lent him the strength to heave the wolf off even as

fangs tore his sleeve and raked his forearm. Rising onto a knee, he shoved the muzzle at its face and sent a slug crashing through its skull.

Fargo spun.

The two remaining wolves had ringed the Ovaro. Snarling and snapping, they leaped at its legs and its belly.

Rearing, the stallion flailed with its heavy hooves and there was the sharp *crack* of splintering bones. The Ovaro kicked out and sent the wolf tumbling.

The last wolf had crouched and waited its chance. Now it saw it. With a powerful bound, it sprang at the Ovaro's unprotected throat.